Hunts in Dreams

Books by Tom Drury

Hunts in Dreams

∽ Tom Drury

HOUGHTON MIFFLIN COMPANY

BOSTON · NEW YORK 2000

For information about permission to reproduce
selections from this book, write to
Permissions, Houghton Mifflin Company,
215 Park Avenue South, New York,
New York, 10003.

Library of Congress Cataloging-in-Publication Data
Drury, Tom
Hunts in dreams / Tom Drury.
    p.   cm.
ISBN 0-395-94113-X
1. Problem families — Middle West — Fiction.
2. Family — Middle West — Fiction. 3. Middle West
— Fiction. I. Title.
PS3554.R84 H56   2000
813'.54 — dc21   99-055519

Printed in the United States of America

Book design by Robert Overholtzer

QUM 10 9 8 7 6 5 4 3 2 1

FOR

CHRISTIAN AND CLAUDIA

AND IN MEMORY OF

MARCELLE IRENE DRURY

1930–1999

✺ Friday

1 · Charles

THE MAN behind the counter of the gun shop did not understand what Charles wanted, and so he summoned his sister from the back room, and she did not understand either. It was late on a Friday afternoon in October, and Charles seemed to be speaking an unknown language.

Outside, the wind gusted. Sunlight broke through fast clouds and swept across the windows. The sister, in a coarsely woven blue sweater, picked up the feeding rod of a semiautomatic rifle and flicked it at her brother's arm in play. Charles thought of it as a feeding rod, anyway. No doubt there was another name.

"On guard," she said.

"I told you," said the brother, "keep away from me with that."

What Charles wanted seemed simple enough to Charles: for the gun-shop owners to visit the minister's widow and offer to buy the shotgun she kept on pegs above the fireplace.

This is the history of the gun: Years ago it had belonged to Charles's stepfather, who before his death had given it to the Reverend Matthews. It was a .410 side-by-side shotgun made by Hutzel and Pfeil of Cincinnati. In his mind Charles could see the company name engraved in ornate script on the breechblock. When the minister died, his widow inherited the gun. Maybe it was sentimental for Charles to want to retrieve it after all this time, and yet he believed a gun should be used once in a while. A gun should be more than an ornament on the wall of someone with no connection to the original owner.

The sister took the feeding rod in both hands as if she meant to twirl it like a baton.

"What do you call that?" said Charles, on the off-chance that a simple exchange of information would set the conversation back on track.

"It's the long spring-loaded insert that pushes shells into the chamber," she said.

"Oh, okay."

"How much do you want for this gun?" said the sister.

"I'm not selling it."

"Well, let me ask you this," said the brother. "Do you have it on you?"

"It's at her house."

"We can't appraise what we can't see," said the sister.

"Where is it again?"

"The minister's widow's house. In Grafton. Her name is Farina Matthews."

The brother shook his head. "You're asking the shop to act as a go-between."

"We tried it once," said the sister. "Ended up in small claims court. It was a total loser for us."

Charles looked at a fox pelt, dusty orange with gray fringe, tacked to the wall of the shop. The fox had been flattened, its paws flung outward. "What I'm suggesting is —"

"Yeah . . ."

"— you go to her, you buy it from her, then you would hold

it free and clear, and then I come in, as if none of this had happened. And I buy it from you."

"We don't make house calls," said the brother. "We're not like doctors."

"Actually we are, in that respect," said the sister. "We're not like old-time doctors, who made house calls."

"If you want to have her stop by the shop, that's a different story."

"She doesn't want to sell it," said Charles. "Not to me, anyway."

"Why is this conversation taking place?" said the brother.

He turned away, presenting the blank white back of his shirt to Charles. Blue gun barrels stood in a row, silver chain laced through the trigger guards. Above the guns there was a license plate — *Iowa 1942* — all beat up as if the car or truck it had been on had hit many stumps. The sister pulled a catalogue from under the counter and began turning the pages.

A lone bluebottle buzzed in the gun shop. "Where did you come from?" said the sister. She raised her hand briefly in the fly's direction before returning to her search. "Okay. Here we go. The gun you want, here it is, Hutzel and Pfeil, and it's . . . umm . . . no longer made."

A pheasant rose from dry weeds by the railroad track, the sound of its wings like the spinning of a wheel. Charles and his stepfather fired almost at once as it passed over the right-of-way. White clouds blazed in the sky. The pheasant fell near the tracks. Which of them had hit it was anyone's guess.

"We'll shoot for it," said Charles's stepfather. "I'll be odd."

Indeed you will, thought Charles. He twisted the bill of his hat. "I don't know how," he said.

His stepfather explained. On the count of three they would each display a number of fingers, letting the even- or oddness of the combined total decide who got the pheasant. Did Charles understand? No, but he pretended to. And sure enough, he did not do it right, presenting his fingers too late and nonetheless making a sum that lost the game.

His stepfather walked on, leaving the pheasant for Charles to carry. "If you're going to take the trouble to cheat," he said, "you should at least win."

They crossed to the cabin through a meadow of grass and mint. They could smell the mint as their steps broke the plants. Birch trees grew around the house, which was made of wood, with a plank door. It did not belong to Charles's stepfather but was open for the use of all. Inside, ants wandered over the walls and the rafters. A river ran far below the windows. The stepfather boiled water on a hot plate while Charles gathered newspapers on which they would clean the pheasant. *Surveyor 6* had lifted off from the moon, only to land again a few feet away.

"I didn't cheat," said Charles.

This would have been the fall of 1967. After that Charles knew how to shoot for something, at least in this limited sense.

The minister's widow pushed a lawn aerator on a line between the clothesline and the house. Three sharp stars turned brightly through the grass. She kept an excellent yard and had always made it a point to do so. A van stopped on the street in front of the house. HERE COMES CHARLES THE PLUMBER was written, red on white, above the grille. She gripped the worn wooden handle of the aerator as if she might pick it up and chase the driver away.

"There is nothing to talk about," she said.

"I've just come from the gun shop," said Charles. "They made an estimate. This is more than fair." From a paper envelope he drew three bills.

"Where did you get that?"

"The bank."

She could have used the money — who couldn't use three hundred now and then? — but resolutely she returned to her work. "Why would I do for payment what I wouldn't do for free?"

He laid the bills on the grass in her path. She speared them deftly with the tines of the aerator. "I'm not selling the gun."

"Why not?"

"Ask your mother."

"I talked to her," said Charles. "She said it was that time with your boy."

"Is that right?"

"When he was in the runaway car."

She raised the aerator and the impaled money. "Are you threatening me?"

Charles took the bills back. "Mrs. Matthews, I'm trying to buy a gun which can't be any use to you. I know I don't have any right to it. But what happened between my mother and you thirty years ago I can't help. Just let me see it."

"Well, you don't have to cry about it."

"Let me see the gun."

"You already did."

In the summer she had let him into the house. Standing before the mantel he had seemed big and misplaced, and she had worried for her miniature lighthouses of painted clay. Clearly he saw things in the gun that she did not, but it had been left to her by her husband, and she meant to keep it.

Farina Matthews climbed the steps of her house and washed her hands at the kitchen sink while watching the white van move down the road. THERE GOES CHARLES THE PLUMBER. She walked through the rooms, past a vase of cloth roses that seemed to watch her. Her husband had called their home Max Gate, after the residence of Thomas Hardy, his favorite author. She did not look at the gun. Her gaze drifted to the piano, on which stood a large and beautifully framed picture of her son. He was a chemist in Albuquerque and had done well for himself, discovering when he was barely out of college a new way of treating synthetic laminate so that it would remember its former shape in a vacuum.

The runaway car business amounted to nothing. That's what Charles would never understand. When her son was four years old, she had left him in the car while getting the mail at the post office. Somehow the youngster had released the brake. The car rolled down the snowy street, but so slowly that her son would never have gotten anywhere. Far from saving him, Charles's mother had made the situation worse by loping alongside the car and shouting as loudly as she could.

And now Charles wanted Farina to sell him the old gun, which complemented her fireplace in such a homey way. When everyone knew he stole and that his plumbing customers were either shady themselves or tolerant of shadiness. *I think not,* said the minister's widow to herself.

Charles Darling lived with his wife Joan, their son Micah, and Joan's daughter Lyris on two acres south of the town of Boris. The house had been built a hundred years ago and added on to forty years ago, and the two pieces did not much match. The older part was a dormered cottage, the newer part a boot room. All in all, the place was too small, especially since the arrival of Lyris, the daughter whom Joan had placed for adoption sixteen years before.

Behind the house stood a stucco hut with a dirt floor. They called it a barn, but this was an overstatement. The doors latched with a hasp and pin, and the soft ruts of the driveway were thick with grass. Railroad tracks ran behind the back yard, and trees grew on the hill beyond the tracks. Charles went into the barn and looked through his toolboxes for a chain pipe wrench. He had no immediate need for it but had noted its absence and did not like to be out and about without it.

In the house he asked Micah if he had taken the wrench from the barn.

"Describe it," said the boy.

"About yay long and blue, with a chain on the end," said Charles. "Like a bike chain. It's a good heavy wrench. You can't mistake it for anything else."

Micah sat on the deep freeze in the boot room looking at a clothespin as if a secret message had been written on it in very small print. The red hair bristled on his head. He had careful, measuring eyes. "What's a bike chain?"

"How old are you?"

"Seven."

"And you're asking me that."

"I didn't take any wrench."

It bothered Charles that Micah could not ride, and yet there was only so much he himself could do. A father can't ride a bike for a son. "You've got to know these things, Mike."

"Do you want to hear my part in the school play?"

"Get off this," said Charles. "Get off a minute."

Micah jumped down from the freezer. Charles raised the lid and pulled up a clouded blue sack of ice. "Let's hear your part in the school play."

"'You know, as well as I / The fossil record does not lie.'"

"What's the topic?" said Charles.

"Evolution."

Charles beat on the ice with a hammer and then made a drink in the kitchen, where Joan sat at the table packing her suitcase for a trip to the city. The orderly stacks of her clothing seemed at odds with the clutter of the kitchen. Curtains lay in heaps under the windows. One of the burners on the stove, missing the knob that turned it on and off, was controlled by a pair of vise grips locked onto the metal stem. Under the table were black suede riding chaps, a green laundry basket with clothes spilling over the sides, and a tin of walnuts. Everything might have been moving a short time before, spinning around Joan and her suitcase.

"Don't say anything," she said. "I'm thinking."

Charles took Micah and the drink outside. The bike leaned against a stone column. Charles turned it upside down so that it rested in the dirt on seat and handlebars, and worked the pedals, blurring the spokes of the rear wheel.

"If you learned how to ride, you would know what the chain was," Charles advised. He righted the bicycle, lifted the boy onto the seat, and gave a push. "Leave now and you can be in Canada by the first snow."

The bicycle wobbled into the cool air of fall. Charles picked up his drink from the ground. Micah could not steady the handlebars but kept wrenching them back and forth in the stylized tango of all beginning riders. Then he fell, on the sand by the road. He disentangled himself from the bike and ran to Charles, holding his elbow, on which blood appeared in dozens of tiny gouges. Charles helped him limp to the house. The boy's breath came at rough intervals. "I don't like learning," he said.

"Learning isn't so bad," said Charles. "It's falling that hurts."

Joan had closed her suitcase. Her arms lay over the lid, her head resting sideways between them, as if she were listening to the heartbeat of the luggage, her blond hair fanned over her shoulders. She looked spent and peaceful, like a pilgrim who has found the sacred site.

She spoke softly into the pale hollow of an elbow. "Did you remember to get my travel-sized samples?"

"I did." Charles reached into the pockets of his coat and laid on the table his keys, the three hundred dollars, and the small containers of face cream and hair conditioner that she would not go without. Joan held reflexive opinions about many subjects, including travel. Everything had to be a certain way long before the time of departure or else she became anxious.

Micah ducked under the table. "Daddy! Here's your wrench." He had found it nestled in the chaps.

"What happened to your elbow?" said Joan. "Oh, Charles, why do you have to roughhouse with him on the very night before I go away?"

"He fell off his bike," said Charles. "Don't read things into it that aren't there."

"And who ends up dressing the wound?"

"Stop arguing," said Micah.

As a rule, Charles and Joan did not let their seven-year-old tell them what to do, but they disagreed often enough lately that they sometimes forgot to remind him of his lack of authority.

Charles sat in a chair, shoving the tin of walnuts with a steel-toed boot to clear space for his feet. The ice of his drink had melted to wafers.

"I would be glad to put a Band-Aid on Micah's arm," he said diplomatically, knowing that Joan would never give up the chance to doctor her son when she was on the verge of going away for the weekend. She was the executive director of a league of animal shelters headquartered in Stone City, and would give a speech at the regional convention on Saturday night.

Joan led Micah upstairs. Charles took the opportunity to raise the lid of her suitcase. Her blouses and skirts, her black swimsuit, lay carefully folded, and under them he found the white Bible with her maiden name printed in gold. He unzipped her flowered cloth makeup bag and removed silver and gold tubes of lipstick, an eyelash curler that looked like some ungodly surgical scissors, and a paintbox for the eyes. Cosmetics bothered Charles. He did not want Joan going to the city with any more makeup than that which was on her face when she left. He did not want her dolling up for strangers in a strange place. Either the men would fall for her or they would not, and she would be left standing alone, with paint masking her pretty features. He buried the makeup in the laundry basket and filled the flowered bag with walnuts and a nutcracker from the tin beneath the table.

Her blouses moved him. Their insubstantiality and frail collars seemed to correspond to something tenuous in Joan's nature. People did not realize what an effort it required for her to simply appear normal, an inhabitant of the regular world. The things she did for work were much more than Charles could have managed. She sat in meetings in clothes unfriendly to the skin. She spoke civilly to people who would just as soon see her fall out of a window so they could take her place. She visited factories, seeking donations, admiring forklifts. She rarely dealt with animals anymore.

Her work life corresponded less and less with her home life. If her board of directors could see this kitchen — the moths that flew from the cupboards or the molasses congealed on the shelves of the refrigerator — their eyes would open wide. "What sort of people live here?" they might ask. But maybe their houses were the same.

A swimsuit, he thought. *Where does that fit in?*

Lyris came home at suppertime. After three months, she still entered the house gravely. She leaned forward, looking for something.

She had arrived on the eleventh of July with a small suitcase of her own. She'd set it down, picked it up, turned it around, considering whether to stay. Charles wondered what she had left behind in the culling of her possessions.

She had her mother's blond hair, chopped short, as if the beauty parlor responsible had been on a boat on the rolling sea. Her eyes were small but did not seem so because her irises were big and dark. *The father's eyes,* Charles had thought, with some jealousy, and just as he was thinking this, Lyris's eyes had met his, and he looked away. With her, that first time, were a man and a woman from the Home Bringers, the organization that had found her in Illinois, informed Joan and Charles of her existence, and brought her home.

Joan had seemed as amazed as Charles by the advent of Lyris. Joan had once been an actress, and she had the requisite ability to set aside the past in favor of any given scenario. She seemed to believe some things that were not true more than she did some things that were. Charles figured this was why she was so susceptible to religion. Once she had told Charles of a problem with the elevator in the building where she worked in Stone City. The car, it seemed, would stop between floors, and the doors would open, revealing the wall of the elevator shaft. It was only later that he found out the building had no elevators. When he pointed out this fact, she said that he had misunderstood, that she had only been telling him what someone else had told her, about another building, in another place. But he knew what he had heard, and he remembered how convincingly she had described the cables and rivets and grease of the shaft. No, she said. He was wrong.

At times like these, Charles thought, it was as if Joan were changing scripts. It took her a moment, but she would go on.

Lyris's father had been an actor; he and Joan had been in a drama workshop together in Chicago back in the eighties. Charles could picture the whole chain of events, inaccurately. Lyris had grown up in an orphanage and foster homes, never finding a lasting situation. There were difficult aspects to her life that the Home Bringers related with apparent joy. Her most recent foster parents had been apprehended with bomb-making equipment; the arrests had brought her to the Home Bringers' attention. So they had delivered her from trouble and given her real mother a chance to correct her mistake. There was no doubt in their minds about being in the right. If there were, they would find another line of work. They were small people, with small hands, representing a movement against what they called artificial families. The only love that counted, they said, was blood love.

Charles thought this was way off. Nonetheless, he and Joan now had two children, although it had once been predicted that they could have none. It made Charles happy when doctors and scientists got caught in a mistake. He cheered their miscalculations. Signals arrive from a space telescope, and lo and behold, there are forty billion more galaxies than there were yesterday. An infertile couple winds up having two children. The scientists must have known the guessing game they were playing. Did they laugh derisively behind laboratory walls; did they roll dice to determine the number of galaxies and grains of sand?

He wondered about those scientists.

Now Joan came downstairs saying that the bathroom was becoming a natural spring. She had that right. Water floated the tiles at the base of the toilet and beaded the coupling under the sink, from which the pearly drops made their way in procession down the elbow trap, off the cleanout, through space, and into an overturned hardhat placed on the floor to catch the water. The hat had tire marks on the crown from a time in Colorado when Charles had driven a car over it to see how hard it really was.

"And the carpenter's children shall go without shoes," said Lyris. She wore a middy blouse and a kilt with a giant safety pin.

"That's *cobbler*," said Charles.

Lyris at sixteen was just as willowy and high-browed as

a princess, and her shape was evident, but Charles looked around it. There were many ways their relationship might go wrong, and he meant to avoid them all. He regarded himself as an innovator with no tolerance for the obvious sins. And Lyris had seen enough of the world's selfish ways. As the song said, she was a poor wayfaring stranger.

Lyris took a head of lettuce from the refrigerator and bit into it as if it were an apple. Charles and Joan exchanged an expression of live-and-let-live. Some of her habits were not what they were used to. She ate raw potatoes, ironed her socks, and drank milk from a bowl.

"How was 4-H?" asked Joan. "Honey? Lyris? Did you make corncob dolls with the rest of the girls?"

Lyris boosted herself up to sit on the edge of the counter. "I feel too old for 4-H. Lots of the kids are nine and ten. I would drop out tomorrow if you would let me."

"I'm going away tomorrow," said Joan. "And there certainly are girls your age in 4-H."

"There's Taffy, who everyone kisses up to. But I can't play that game."

"Lyris."

"They do! 'Look at my corncob doll, Taffy.' 'What big eyes you have, Taffy.' With that name, I can't take her seriously."

"It's short for Octavia," said Joan.

"You should get a goat to raise and show at the fair," said Charles. "That's where the real benefits of 4-H begin to kick in. With livestock."

"Could I really have a goat?" said Lyris.

"I don't know why not," said Charles.

"Do I really want a goat?"

"Health, hands, head," said Charles. "What's the other H?"

"Heart," said Lyris.

Micah braced himself on the banister and leaped up in outrage. Why could she get a goat when he couldn't have a dog, he wanted to know. It was so unfair. He could not believe how unfair it was.

"Goats are like dogs except they don't bite," said Charles. A German shepherd had bit him once on the knee when he had surprised it in a garage.

"Can we not talk about animals right now?" said Joan. "I'll be doing that all weekend. Now let me think. I'm leaving at six in the morning. That means I have to fill up my tank and check the oil and fluid levels and vacuum the mats tonight."

"But you're flying," said Charles.

"To the airport I'm not," said Joan.

"Where's the doll you made?" Micah asked Lyris. He hung on the railing, his elbow bound in gauze.

"I tossed it," said Lyris.

"I was hoping to put it in my Playmobil prison."

"You are a cop in your heart," said Lyris.

"Lyris called me a cop," said Micah.

"She didn't mean it," said Charles. "But you shouldn't go around threatening to imprison your sister's doll. As for the goat, you can help with it, assuming we get one."

"You can put it in a *pen*," said Lyris.

Two combines worked a field from opposite sides. Night would fall in an hour. Charles's brother, Jerry, was driving to Boris from Pringmar. He passed an irrigation reservoir with a round island of evergreens in the middle. It occurred to him that the trees' lives must be like his own in some ways, though not, fortunately, in others. In town he pulled over by the teen center, where Octavia Perry and some of her friends loitered by the pay phone. The same Taffy who exhibited model 4-H behavior was now smoking and standing with her belly thrust forward and one hand pressed into the small of her back.

"Where's the party?" asked Jerry.

"We don't know yet," said Octavia. "Wait a minute, Mr.

Postman." Jerry delivered mail for a living. His pith helmet lay on the seat beside him.

"Look what I got for you," said Jerry. He opened his glove-box and took out a small black chessboard with magnetic pieces. "Pawn to queen four," he said.

Octavia responded with a mirror move of her queen's pawn. Several moves later, the phone rang in the booth.

"Will he cling to the pawn or let it go?" said Taffy. She wedged the cigarette between her thumb and the tip of her middle finger and fired it into the gutter.

One of Taffy's companions hung up the phone. "The Elephant," he said. "It's at the Elephant."

This was a traditional party site out in the country, named for a formation of trees whose shape against the sky had once been found to resemble the profile of an elephant. The likeness, if any, had given way to the growth of branches. The party would be in a meadow below the trees.

"Bishop to queen's knight five would be a big mistake," said Jerry.

"Oh *really*," said Taffy. "Look, I don't want to play if you're going to take me for a novice. Are you coming to the party or not?"

"Will there be a keg?" said Jerry.

"*Es claro que sí.*"

The evening sky had rolled like a bolt of blue cloth over the town. Jerry gazed at the cloudy shine of the little pearls in Octavia's earlobes. "Probably what I'll do is go on home and check out the Discovery Channel."

"You're an old man," said Taffy.

"A blanket drawn 'round my shoulders," said Jerry.

"I'm not in love with you."

"A cup of cheer, to while away the hours."

"I'm not in love," said Taffy.

From the town Jerry drove to Charles and Joan's house.

Joan sat on the front porch shining her shoes, and Charles lay on a wheeled wooden slab under Joan's car, the front tires of which were up on steel ramps.

"Evening, folks," said Jerry.

"I'm going away," called Joan.

"Joanie, we hardly knew ye."

"Only for the weekend," she said, holding a chamois cloth to the fading light. "It's work-related."

"Then I don't want to hear it," said Jerry. "Charles, I need your help over home. I got some rock salt that has to go down in the cellar."

Soon Charles and his brother were speeding down the road with the evening wind blowing bits of paper and dust around the inside of the car. Jerry explained his plan, which had nothing to do with rock salt. He wanted to fake a police raid on the party at the Elephant. As a postman, he had revolving lights behind his windshield; as a volunteer fireman, he carried a bullhorn. Jerry liked to spoil fun; it was his latest hobby. Once Micah had rigged a tent out of old canvas and a clothesline strung between two trees, and Jerry had pulled out a buck knife and cut the rope, sending the heavy canvas thudding to the ground. He had also taken to making bothersome phone calls to people who advertised cars for sale in the classifieds. "Is it a manual or a stick?" he would ask, usually late at night, just to play with their heads.

Jerry pulled off the road and into the trees that constituted the Elephant. Down in the meadow, shadowy figures moved back and forth among the cars. "La Grange" came from someone's stereo.

"They play the same songs we played," said Charles idly.

"I know it." Jerry put the car in gear. "There's no sense of musical progression." The car rolled out of the woods and down the slope toward the party, yellow light revolving.

"Stay away from your cars," said Charles into the bullhorn, but there was no amplification.

"You've got to push the button. And say *vehicles*."

"Stay away from your vehicles." Now Charles's words echoed over the meadow to the opposite hillside. "Do not start the engines. Do not drive away."

The lazy party flared to life. Kids ran, doors slammed, headlights cut yellow swaths through the darkness. Dust rose as the fishtailing caravan hit the road. It was good to create so much panic, but at the same time Charles suspected that the young people were having more fun than he was.

Jerry rode the brakes, giving everyone time to get away. He parked the car, and they both got out and took a handcart from the trunk. The kids had abandoned the keg in a ring of matted grass. Charles lifted the cold aluminum barrel onto the cart, Jerry cinched the cloth straps, and they took turns pulling the cart uphill to the car.

"I wonder why they left it," said Charles.

"You know kids," said Jerry. "Always in a hurry."

2 · Lyris

LYRIS REMEMBERED the sign in the orphanage cafeteria: AND HAVING FOOD AND RAIMENT, LET US BE THEREWITH CONTENT. This made a certain amount of sense. She tried to remember more — the cheap forks and how easily they bent, the gallery from which the headmistress watched the orphans, the oppressive hairnets of the cooks — but found it hard to do so with clarity. She felt too young to be forgetting.

She stood in her bedroom watching the road as Joan drove off for the gas station. Charles had gone somewhere with Jerry. Micah was downstairs playing a video game called El Mono, in which a monkey ran and jumped to evade an army of flying skulls. Lyris could hear the shrill monotonous cries of the monkey.

The corncob doll was in her backpack. What she'd said about throwing it out was untrue. She retrieved it now and lay down on her bed. The beads and cloth and Styrofoam head tore away easily. So much for the doll. The red of the bare shelled cob was not the same as any red she had known. It was like the color of blood but rustier. Maybe dried blood. That could be it. It was nearly as light as air, this dried, natural thing. A few yellow kernels remained, probably a dozen in all. Their placement seemed random but significant, with a meaning she could not read.

She played around with the corncob for a while. She lobbed it from hand to hand, scratched her temple, brushed her hair. It was a novelty to her. She spoke into it as if it were a microphone.

"It's moonlight," she said.

The phrase came from a roller rink where she used to go with her foster sister Lorna. Lorna was the daughter of her first and best foster parents. Lyris and Lorna had gone round and round the rink holding hands. It turned out, however, that skating was easier if you did not hold hands. So after falling several times, they let go. The rink was lit by white floodlights that sometimes shut down dramatically, leaving only the dark glow of blue spotlights to play over the thin wooden strips of the floor. Then, in a glass booth above the skaters, the man who played the music would lean close to the microphone and say, "It's moonlight."

It ended with Lorna's parents because their clothing store went bankrupt.

The parents in her second foster home were an older couple who were basically looking for someone to work around their house. The man had a spot on his forehead that looked like a map of Florida. Sometimes Lyris thought the placement people had allowed him to become a foster father only because they wanted to show they were not put off by that spot. Lyris was there for part of the year she turned twelve. The state took her back after she broke her arm carrying an air conditioner down a flight of stairs.

The third couple with whom Lyris lived would have to be considered the most affluent. They had several recreational vehicles and liked to go out in the country to drive their Jeep on the rough ground below the power lines. The fun of this escaped Lyris. It felt like being in a can that someone was kicking. She would later wonder if her inability to enjoy the off-road experience had contributed to the couple's decision to stop being foster parents.

Last before Charles and Joan had been Pete and Jackie. They were the ones who were found with bomb materials. Lyris had her ups and downs with them. When she became convinced, after having a dream in which she saw Lorna riding a wolf, that her former foster sister had died, they tried to help. After doing all they could to convince her that dreams reflect worries rather than realities, Pete and Jackie took Lyris to see Lorna. The visit did not go well. The family had moved, they were no longer bankrupt, and they seemed to want nothing to do with their old life. Lorna was with a group of friends who looked at Lyris as if to say, "What's this supposed to be?"

Pete made it easy for the police to learn of his involvement with bombs, even going so far as to name his dog after an explosive. "Here, Cordite," he would call, with darkness settling on the suburb where they lived. "Come home, Cordite." The dog, a strong and dim-witted Dalmatian, would run all over the neighborhood, dragging his muddy stake on a rope.

What a scene it had been when the police raided the house. They smelled something burning and believed the place might erupt in flames at any time. It was really just an old iron that Lyris had plugged in, intending to press her jeans. Two men came crashing up the stairs, grabbed her away from the ironing board, and carried her down so that her feet never touched the ground. She would always remember the racket of their shoes on the stairs. Over the banister she got a look at her wrinkled jeans.

That night she was interrogated by both the police and the Home Bringers. She got to eat at a desk while they asked questions.

"Do you go to school?"

"Do I come across as someone who does not?"

"Were you ever asked to deliver a package to someone and you didn't know what was inside?"

"No sir."

"More fries?"

"No, thank you."

"Would you like to live with your mother?"

"Who is she?"

"An actress."

"Would I have seen her in anything?"

"She was fired from a play the fall before you were born. That's as much as we've been able to find out. Playing a pregnant woman."

"You mean that at the same time —"

"Ironical, isn't it?"

Lyris dropped the corncob beside the bed and moved her hands above her in graceful patterns that she thought might be "of the ballet." In the orphanage the counselors had stressed the worth and sanctity of the body, as if the orphans were not discarded children but athletes in training. Tumbling was mandatory, twice daily; there were many proficient tumblers. Days were full and nights were free. What peace there could be at the orphanage once the lights were out, breaths slowing until they became one sound.

Was it so bad? she asked herself now. *All in all, no, not so bad.*

One of the good points of Lyris's room at Charles and Joan's house was that she could walk out the window onto the roof of the boot room. She did this now and straddled the ridge. It was nearly dark, but she could still make out the shapes of the open country and of the trees around the house. Through the windows of the barn she saw a light. It could be that elf Micah with a flashlight. He adored Charles, but he did everything possible to bug him.

When she went downstairs she found Micah still there, hypnotized by El Mono, who was trapped in a tree.

"I'm going outside," she said. "Boy! Do you hear me?"

He nodded slowly and shifted his weight on the davenport. An apple core rolled slowly over the cushion. Lyris picked up the core. "Look at this," she said.

"You can finish it."

"How will I ever repay you?"

"You don't have to."

She ate the core and stem on the way to the barn. Inside, the last rays of the sun were striking the brass fittings of a steamer trunk and reflecting on the walls. She turned around to look outside. A blanket of blue-black clouds had compressed the evening light to a deep yellow band on the horizon. She threaded her way through wooden boxes and stout-handled tools and coiled chains to the trunk, which was pushed against the back wall of the barn. It was not locked. Inside were hats, shoes, dresses, and coats from Joan's acting days. Lyris was wearing cutoffs and the middy blouse, and over these she pulled on a green velvet dress with full, floating sleeves and a black collar. Yellow fabric lined the sleeves and vertical pockets. She sat down in a threadbare upholstered rocking chair and tried on a pair of black fabric shoes. They had high heels and serrated gold leaves woven over the toes. Everything seemed a perfect fit. She closed her eyes and let her head tip back. Perhaps remnants of Joan's line of thinking resided in her old clothes and would seep from them into Lyris's mind. Then she might understand. She breathed deep and waited. *I'll be okay with whatever it is,* she thought. In time she saw a billboard for suntan lotion rising from waving clover. Children walked through the field chewing the sweet white tips of the flowers. Not very specific. She rearranged the folds of the dress over her legs. Then the barn doors banged shut and the pin rattled down into the lock.

A young man named Follard walked through the woods carrying a metal detector. He wore a hardhat with a headlamp that jostled back and forth. Follard liked working after nightfall, because no one else did. Metal detecting had become quite the popular hobby, and Follard regarded his competition with disdain. Mostly they were doing the same thing he was doing, but it seemed reasonable to assume that nightfall separated the metal men from the hobbyists. The very word *hobbyist* made him shudder. He was twenty-two but looked older. There were wrinkles around his eyes. The narrowness of his head seemed likewise to suggest an older man, whittled and honed by the troubles of many years. The metal detector featured a plastic cuff that nearly closed around his right forearm like the fitting of a crutch. Completing the outfit was a folding shovel, obtained from a military surplus store, that rode in a holster on his hip.

He carried his metal detector with a seasoned authority that might have made metal leap out of the ground in his presence. Cows roamed the woods during the day, eating the groundcover between the trees; they made paths that ran in every direction.

Geese passed overhead, faintly calling. Follard could sense their heavy bodies above the branches. Coming over a rise, he saw red taillights across the grass of the old WPA road. He turned off the light on his hat, set the metal detector on mute, and walked up behind a car idling in the road. The couple inside turned in their seats. Perhaps they had already seen the light. When he opened the driver's door, a dope cloud drifted out with its overpowering, mindless fragrance. Follard disliked marijuana, for it had never given him any feeling other than disorientation. It made him suspicious. He held a low opinion of dopers, who had conversations such as the following, which he'd once overheard:

"When you think about radio — it's just — the waves, I mean — in every corner of the sky — and you can't *see* them? — and they're all coming through the roof of your house, these invisible . . . hoops or whatever — if you explained it to someone but without using, you know, the word *radio,* they'd go, 'Not likely.'"

"Like the Declaration of Independence."

"Exactly."

"'Cause when you read it to people but you don't say what it is — I seen this once on TV — and they didn't say what it was —"

"I seen that too! They were on street corners."

"I forget where they were. But no one would sign their name to it. They thought it was a Communist manifesto. Or it might have been something else."

A boy and a girl from a nearby town stepped out of the car. They knew Follard, and if they were wary of him, they also seemed relieved that he was not a cop. The girl was crying and wiping her eyes with the heels of her hands. She explained that she had lost her class ring at the Elephant. The two had been at a party that was broken up by the police, and in the confusion her ring had slipped from her finger. It was white gold with an amethyst stone.

Other people's troubles tended to aggravate Follard. He was selfish in that way. The girl gestured erratically and the boy just stood there, holding a carved wooden pipe.

"Have you tried looking for it?" said Follard.

"We had to leave," said the boy. "All these cop cars were swarming down. And when we went back, the keg was gone."

The girl blew her nose with an embroidered handkerchief. "Why bother?" she said disconsolately. "When we know we'll never find it. It cost a lot of money." Remembering the price, she began crying again.

"Better to light a candle than curse the darkness," said Follard.

"My parents will ground me until Thanksgiving," said the girl.

The boy laughed, and both the girl and Follard looked at him. "I'm sorry," he said. "That was inappropriate." He set the wooden pipe between his teeth, lifted the girl into a seated position on the fender of the car, and rubbed her shoulders.

"What the fuck's funny about that, Ronnie?" she said.

Follard let them go back and forth a while longer and then told two stories from his life. He had good stories, full of violence and breakage. The boy and girl had heard these particular ones before, but they listened respectfully, for Follard was older than they were and had lived on his own since the age of fourteen. He had a place in Stone City that the entire high school knew of simply as "the house on the corner." The first story concerned a fire he had escaped, and the second involved someone he knew chasing people at a birthday party with the leg of a broken chair.

"And look at me now," said Follard in conclusion. "A life of perfect freedom. I come. I go. I hunt metal all hours of the night if I want. And I do want. I could find that ring."

"That really work?" said Ronnie.

"Give me something metal."

The boy dug in his pockets. "I got a quarter."

"It don't work with quarters."

"I got a pocketknife."

"Let me see," said Follard, turning on his headlamp. It was a brushed steel knife with a flying pheasant painted on the housing. Follard threw it into the trees beyond the car.

He handed the metal detector to the boy. "Go on up there

listening for the signal. And don't mess with my settings."

Ronnie started to say something but then fitted his arm into the cuff and walked away with the disk of the metal detector leading the way. He seemed pleased to be trusted with Follard's device. He would never find the knife.

"Hey, Suzanne," said Follard.

"Suzette." The girl slid backward on the hood of the car.

"Now you both lost something."

The girl folded her handkerchief and put it in the pocket of her jacket. "Scat, you big old alley cat," she said.

Lyris waited for her eyes to adjust to the dark. All she could see were the six square windows, dimly gray, over the barn doors. She kicked the shoes from her feet, and they landed with sharp quick sounds like those of a small animal. Best not to think of small animals. She stepped on something, lost her balance, bumped a toolbox, sent it crashing to the floor. She shut her eyes so that pinwheels of light turned slowly behind her lids. She tried to take off the dress, but the train was snagged and her efforts only pulled her backward. She was a little afraid, breathing too fast. The dress pulled free, pitching her into a sawhorse, over which she fell, headlong, shielding her face with her hands. Her wrist hit the engine housing of an electric generator, and she calculated at once that the bruise would be deep and lasting. The fallen sawhorse dug painfully into her belly and shins. She lay panting for a long time, got up, and moved to the doors. They were locked and would not give. A metal rod ran the length of each door, below the windows. She jumped once and then again, caught the rusted rod in her hands, and pulled herself up until she could see through the glass. It was only then that she realized what had closed the barn doors. Her experiment in thought transference had not done it — it was Micah, who stood on the grass before the doors with his fingers in his ears, his eyes glinting like a cat's.

"Let me out of here, you little fuckhead," she cried.

"I can't."

She dropped and felt around for the handle of a sledge or an axe. "You better think of a way," she called, her hands sweeping the dirt floor in even arcs. "Actually, you migh's well not," she muttered, "because I am going to hurt the hell out of you one way or another."

Eventually her right hand closed over the mud-crusted handle of a spade. Her breath came in harsh bursts, as if she had been sprinting. "Open the door," she screamed. She stood, set the point of the spade in the space between the doors. Of course they did not fit tightly together; nothing did in this place to which she had been assigned. "Get out of the way, Micah."

Lyris lifted the handle of the spade to her shoulder, as an archer would raise her bow, thrust the point between the doors, and with her bruised hands swung the handle hard and to the left. The spade shaft bowed and a band of pressure stretched the width of the barn. Wood creaked and splintered, the doors broke open, and Lyris staggered into the open. The moon shone through a maze of clouds. She flung the spade down so hard that it stood in the driveway. Micah wrapped his arms around her waist and buried his head in the velvet front of the dress. He spoke words she could not understand. Against her will she found herself rubbing his narrow back so that he almost disappeared in the sleeves.

"It's all right, boy."

Micah lifted his head. "I couldn't help you, Lyris. I locked you in but I couldn't unlock you. I don't know why."

"It's all right," she told him. "I'm going to get you, but not when you're expecting it."

"It's all my fault."

"It sure is."

He took the dress in his hands. "You'd better put this away before Mom gets home."

Lyris shushed Micah, thinking someone was near.

Follard had drifted away from his path in order to trace the submerged shape of an old garbage dump. All the farms used to have them, but the county had issued an edict years ago requiring that they be graded over. The metal detector went crazy when you were on top of one. In Follard's experience these sites were not especially worth digging into, unless you were obsessed, as many were, with blue glass bottles of no value, but still he found it interesting simply to know where they were. He could tune the detector to screen out worthless metals, but usually he didn't. In his mind he was developing a junk map of the lower county.

He had heard smashing and yelling, which told him he was coming up to someone's place. He crossed the railroad tracks and stood in the yard watching the interesting show: the boy standing hypnotized, the doors cracking open, the young woman stumbling out in a long dress. Now he made his entrance, with the hat pushed back on his head, the metal detector slung over his shoulder.

"Hello," he called. "I'm a little lost here. My car must be down the road. My name is Follard."

The girl moved to the back porch and turned on a light. She looked him up and down. Her short blond hair was slick with sweat, and the folds of the green dress were gathered in her hands.

"I look for metal," said Follard, to break her silence.

"We don't have any."

"In the ground, I mean," said Follard. "I find metal in the

ground. Look what I got tonight." He opened his hand to reveal the steel jackknife with the pheasant painting.

"It's pretty," said the girl.

"I thought so."

"What is it?" said the boy.

"A knife," said Follard. "I'll give it to your sister and she can do with it as she sees fit." To Lyris he said, "You look like you've had a rough day. Your dress is torn, if you don't mind my saying it."

The girl gave no encouraging sign, but she did take the knife, as he expected she would.

3 · Joan

THE MAN IN CHARGE of the gas station wore a green button that said

Jim
I Am Empowered
To Serve
You.

This made Joan think, as she had more and more lately, that something was happening to the country. It no longer had the solid feel of any place she was used to. Just the other night a man called the house to say that Joan's family had been chosen from many potential applicants to receive a loan with which to pay down their debt. She pointed out that her family did not have any debt to speak of and that a loan, which was itself debt, could not be very accurately said to pay debt down. The caller replied that he was only reading what was put before him and that he did not wish to argue about the wording, which was not his.

"The pump won't work," she told Jim.

He was sawing open a cardboard box with a utility knife.

Whether he was hostile or simply dedicated to his work was not for Joan to decide. Inside the box were cartons upon cartons of cigarettes.

"When you put the credit card in, pull it out fast," he said. "That's what most people do wrong. They wait around and nothing happens."

"I'm paying cash," she said. "I'm just topping off my tank because tomorrow morning I have to drive to the airport. Can I pay you?"

The man frowned, a carton of Pall Malls in either hand. "After you pump, you can. Otherwise we don't know how much you're taking. And that's nothing against you personally, but these days I'm afraid you have to suspect the worst of everyone. Treat them all as criminals and hope that somehow you might be wrong. To pay cash, here's what you do: put in your card, and the pump will ask you 'Cash or credit?' and you push 'Cash.'"

"I didn't bring a card," said Joan.

"Well, then it's even simpler. All you have to do is push 'Cash' and then it will ask you 'Credit or cash?' and you push 'Cash' and 'Enter' simultaneously."

"I did that," said Joan. "I thought I did."

"What'd the readout say?"

"What's that?"

"It's the gray thing that gives you instructions."

"I don't know."

"Obviously you're not doing it right." The man shoved the cigarette cartons into slots behind the counter.

"Can you help me?"

"I can't leave the store," said the man. "There is a toll-free number you can call."

"Are you empowered to serve me or not?" said Joan.

"Well, I'm not supposed to, but I've seen you around. Just hold on a minute."

Eventually the attendant pumped her gas and she paid. "Thank you, Jim," she said.

On the way out of Chesley she saw thin white smoke climbing from the eaves of the house of a physician named Stephen Palomino. A ladder stood against the house, a half-timbered sprawl with a roof of red tile. Palomino himself was hurrying from the garage wheeling a hose trolley. Joan stopped the car in the road and got out.

"What is it, Steve?" she said.

Dr. Palomino parked the hose by a faucet on the side of the house. "I was stripping paint with a heat gun and now I think the house is on fire." He dropped to the grass and groped for the coupling.

"Go up with the hose," said Joan. "I'll do this."

She knelt and screwed the brass fitting onto the faucet as the doctor climbed the ladder. With her right hand gripping the valve of the faucet, she looked up and said, "Here it comes."

The doctor fired a pistol nozzle at the overhang of the roof, but the spray was too fine.

"Take that off," said Joan as cold water rained on her face. "Steve! Get rid of the nozzle!"

The hose twisted as the doctor wrenched the nozzle back and forth. "Clockwise, counterclockwise, I have no fucking idea," he said, as if to himself. Joan was surprised to hear such language coming from a general practitioner, although come to think of it, she had heard him swear before. She looked away, and then the nozzle fell down and struck her on the shoulder.

"Sorry," yelled the doctor, disappearing in smoke.

Joan rubbed her shoulder, waiting for the cloud to subside. "This is more like it," said Dr. Palomino. "I'm going to drench the wood thoroughly."

Joan looked at her car sitting in the road, lights on and motor running. She hoped that the fire had not penetrated the walls of the doctor's fine old house. The heat gun lay on the grass by the hostas. Her teeth rattled involuntarily. At this moment everything seemed precarious. She wondered why random events sometimes carried so much meaning. Sheets of water ran down the wall. Then the doctor descended the ladder and helped her to her feet. He had tucked the end of the hose into the eaves trough so the water could run unattended.

"I'm glad you happened by," said Dr. Palomino. "This is the second time we've helped each other."

He meant the tornado they had survived years back, when Micah was three. The story made the newspapers because of the way the twister had blown Charles's van, with Joan, Dr. Palomino, and Micah inside, through the wall of a silo. They rarely spoke about this now — it was embarrassing somehow — and Joan decided to think of it some other time.

"Forget heat guns," she said. "Use chemical strippers."

He kicked the gun into the plants. "I'm surprised they can even sell the damned things," he said. "You'd think they'd be looking at a string of liability actions from sea to shining sea, if this is what happens. Of course, you have to use it right. But I can't for the life of me think of anything I was doing that wasn't strictly by the book."

"Did you get my test results?" said Joan.

He closed his eyes. How many test results did he see on a given day? "I did. I did. And they're nothing to worry about, as we say. Your swollen glands are just that — the temporary result of something."

"That's what I was hoping," said Joan. "I can still feel them."

Dr. Palomino touched both sides of her neck. "Let's get you started on an antibiotic. There are some little blue ones I've been meaning to try. Right now, though, I need a drink. Are you going to be home tomorrow? I'll bring a prescription over. I've always wondered where you live."

"I'm going away for the weekend," said Joan.

"Where will you be? I can call, or I can fax."

She felt odd about naming the city and the hotel but reminded herself that he was her doctor and that everything should be aboveboard. The last thing she wanted was to be overtaken by some illness away from home. No doubt the prescription could be filled at some nearby pharmacy or perhaps at the hotel itself. She told him where she would be.

He repeated the name of the hotel — the Astrid — and said that he had never stayed there but had heard good things. She found his endorsement a little annoying. And then, as she turned to her car, he said the oddest thing. At least she thought he did, because she did not quite catch the remark, but it may have been "Oh, Joan, when are we going to get it on?" When she glanced back at the doctor he was turning the crank of the trolley to take up the slack in the hose. Joan drove away, puzzling over his comment, but realized with a reassuring laugh that what he had probably said was "Ah, Joan, *how* are we going to get *along*?" He must have been referring somehow to the unpredictable world in which they lived — a world in which small fires were ignited by accident and put out in haste and confusion — and nothing more.

When one is going away, it is normal to make some fleeting effort to help one's partner. Even if nothing comes of it, the attempt settles the mind a bit for the departure, cleans the slate on which independent adventures may be written. So it was that Joan swung by Charles's mother's house in Boris after helping the doctor put out the fire in his eaves trough. That she suspected some token of intimacy had passed between herself and the doctor only made her more determined to act on

Charles's behalf. Then they would be even, although Charles would know about neither the possible remark nor its resolution in her mind.

Joan knocked on Colette's door and watched through the glass as the old woman made her way across the room. Her hair was wild and white, and she carried a small iron dumbbell in one hand. Colette was known for having had three husbands die, as if this gloomy coincidence had brought her to a rare plane of existence, which maybe it had.

She's the real thing, thought Joan, although she did not know what thing she meant.

"Come in," said Colette. "I spent the day pulling up tomato plants and laying them on the brush pile, even though they've got the order on me not to."

"Who does?"

Colette gestured vaguely with the hand that held the weight. "The town. They say it's unsightly. But you can't get anybody to come in here to take away brush. You can call them, and they say they'll come, they'll take a look, but they never do, why would they."

"Charles and I would."

"Why don't you come tomorrow?"

"Tomorrow's no good."

"Well, make it soon. I'd like to get shook of it."

She returned to her armchair and began raising and lowering the dumbbell. She asked if Joan had seen farmers in the fields on her way and then reminisced about how the combine had done away with the practice of tying corn into sheaves. The older women of the towns still measured their years by what the farmers were doing. Often there was a farm in their family history, and nearly as often that farm had disappeared into bigger operations. Abandoned houses were common, leaning toward the ground. These women must have known, as everyone did, that the towns had been cut loose from this condensed vitality, that the sowing and reaping taking place a mile away could be situated in the fields of California for all the good it did the towns. But Joan guessed they just chose not to think about it. And this made sense in a way, for by the time the towns were gone, these women would be too.

Joan said a prayer in her head: "Let the light fall equally on Colette as on her son and grandson and on Lyris, too. Let me underestimate not a single one, nay, let my faults be as visible to me as if they were under klieg lights. Grant that Meals on Wheels shall not be phased out but shall receive generous underwriting in our handful of days under the sun. Amen."

Joan steered the conversation away from farming and gradually toward the gun that had belonged to Charles's stepfather. Colette recounted the saving of the minister's son. This was an old story to Joan, but she listened again. Colette could not understand after all these years how she had managed to catch up to the rolling car without slipping on the snowy street and falling under the wheels. She had put herself in danger, but it had been nothing more than she hoped anyone would have done for her children, Jerry, Tiny, and Bebe.

Tiny had been Charles's nickname until eight years ago, when he had decided to put childish things aside. (It had to be eight years, because Micah was seven.) Joan had helped him choose which form of his given name he would use in this mature phase of his life. It seemed to Joan that in few decisions of such importance does the individual have complete freedom to choose, and so she had bidden him to take his time. Chuck was too stark, Charlie sounded like someone younger, Chas was out of the question . . . Charles it would be. And it was not long after Charles took his new name that Joan became pregnant with Micah. Experts would discount the connection, but Joan didn't care, she considered nomenclature of the utmost importance. *My name is Legion: for we are many.*

Colette was still talking. There was a misunderstanding of how Charles had come to be called Tiny in the first place. This Joan had not heard before, and she told Colette to hold the story while she made coffee, as her eyes had chosen that moment to begin to ache for the want of caffeine.

Colette put down her weight and offered to make it herself, but Joan insisted, for she knew from experience what thin coffee her mother-in-law brewed. Colette could not help it; she had been born during the Depression, and lived still with remnants of a harsh childhood spent on the plains. A thirteen-ounce can of coffee lasted her weeks and weeks.

Joan went out to the kitchen to make the coffee. By the time she returned, Colette had fallen asleep. Joan touched her arm, and Colette stirred, ready to take up her story.

Charles's stepfather had been drinking whiskey that night. He wandered outside to look at the sunset, leaving his glass half full on a TV table. When they found Charles, he was sitting on the floor beside three rubber lions and the empty glass. He was four years old at the time. Colette picked up the glass and asked Charles if he had drunk from it. The boy reached for the lions and said, "Family," because he saw the three animals as mother, father, and cub.

Colette knelt beside Charles. "Did you drink from the glass?" she asked again.

"Tiny," he said. "It's tiny."

No one but Colette knew what he meant. The whiskey had tasted like metal, like the tines of a fork.

"*Tiney,* he was saying, don't you see?" Colette said. "Not *tiny.* Anyway, that's the most I could make of it."

"Poor little Charles," said Joan.

"He was hammered," said Colette. "But he wasn't little. Even then he was a good solid boy."

Joan gulped coffee. "What do you think about the gun? Maybe if you talked to Farina Matthews."

And say what? Colette wanted to know. She had never gone begging to her neighbors and was not about to begin at this late date.

Dr. Palomino wandered through the cool hallways of his house, drinking scotch from a glass. He stood for a long time in the attic. The air was a little smoky. His family was out of town, having gone to see a production of *Peter Pan*. The water made a full and steady sound as it ran in the eaves trough. The doctor wondered whether he had actually asked that risky closing question or only considered it. But Joan had looked back; he'd said it all right. A doctor could not keep quiet — giving opinions was the essence of medical practice. Still, there was no need to give opinions on whom to get it on with, especially these days, when one never knew when one would be hauled before some hastily assembled review board. But if anyone would understand his carelessness in time of crisis, it would be Joan. The house had been on fire and he had let down his guard. He absolved himself, decided to move on.

Expectation gathered in his chest, ascended, and expanded in the hollow of his head. He had a destination, and the place seemed to know he did. Bookhaven sent a homing signal from across town: *Come to me, Dr. Palomino.* Resistance was necessary, it was part of the fun. Like a mummy called from the tomb, he walked, dragging bandages. Actually, he drove. Bookhaven was a pornographic book store run by a married couple named Gus and Loretta. The windows were painted hospital green. The doctor wore sunglasses and enjoyed the pathetic disguise as he prowled along the gauntlet of bright skin magazines. Never heavy, the doctor felt lighter still in the shop of filthy publications. Gus set up the projector in the back room, thirty dollars for the half-hour. What was thirty dollars to a doctor? Once he saw a four-thousand-dollar telescope on television, picked up the phone, and took delivery the next day. He used it once, to look at a cardinal on the clothesline.

The film was called *Sandra's Teeth*. He had seen it many times.

It is a silent film. A woman wearing a sundress sits in the waiting room of a dentist's office. This is Sandra. A receptionist looks up and speaks. The screen fills with printed words, white on a black background: *What's the problem, miss?* Sandra smiles, revealing teeth so perfect they emit light. The receptionist's eyes widen as she backs away from the desk, overturning her chair. It is all a little overdone. It is supposed to be overdone. She edges along the wall, disappears through a doorway. Sandra closes her mouth without losing the smile. Her eyes are calm and lustrous, and her hands settle in her lap.

Joan and Lyris were standing by the car in the dark when Micah came out to apologize for locking Lyris in the barn. He cried easily, so he would never be disturbed about anything for very long. Then it was Lyris's turn to confess: she had worn a dress from Joan's trunk and torn it, and she had broken the doors. Joan regarded her children fondly. *Subconscious resentment*, she thought. *They are piling it on because I'm leaving.* Yet she luxuriated in her capacity to forgive, to set their troubled minds to rest. Never does a person have so much power as when absolving children of their errors. Some parents, she knew, let the guilt of the children be, let it fester; how foolish they were to forfeit the chance. And children, of course, had very little capacity to release a parent's guilt. It was a weight they could not manage. She put her arms around their shoulders and shepherded them to the house. Micah slipped away to play El Mono. The green dress lay by the suitcase on the kitchen table.

"I wore this in a workshop production of *Into the Quagmire*," Joan told Lyris. "'But what about me? When does my time come? When, Mr. Johnson? Tomorrow? The day after? In a fortnight?' That was my big speech. Your father played the role of Mr. Johnson."

"What was he like?"

"He had a graceful way of getting around the stage," said Joan. "He would be in one place, and then he would be in another, just like that. He had false teeth, from a childhood injury. He was an idealist. He said he would never own property."

"Did he know that I was born? Did he come and see me?"

Joan closed the tear in the sleeve so that the yellow backing could no longer be seen beneath the green. "He came to see you. But there was a documentary filming in Calgary and he had to go away."

"What was it about?"

"I forget. Hydroelectric power or something like that."

"Why didn't you keep me?"

Joan took Lyris's hands in her own. "'Lo, I have sinned, and I have done wickedly: but these sheep, what have they done?'"

"Tell me in your words."

"I'd rather not." She released her daughter's hands. "I mean, there are things I could say, and they're probably even true, but they would sound false, saying them now. That I was young and alone, that I was mixed up — where do I get off saying such things? 'Sinned' and 'done wickedly' cover the subject pretty well."

They sat for a long time without talking. Then Joan picked up her suitcase and carried it toward the door. "I'm sorry," she said.

"A man came through the yard tonight," said Lyris. "He had a metal detector and he'd been in the woods."

Joan turned. "An old man?"

"No."

"You be careful."

"I didn't mean to ruin your dress."

"We can fix it. Don't worry. Anything in that trunk is yours to wear."

"Where'd you get it all?"

"When I left the theater, they told me to take whatever I wanted," said Joan. "I guess it was their way of thanking me."

Actually, she had taken the clothes without asking. But she couldn't in good conscience tell her daughter that.

The dentist wears a white coat and thick black glasses. He directs Sandra to stand on a scale while he takes pictures. She hesitates, covering her mouth with her hands, but then loses her shyness. The dentist clicks away with a box camera. He works urgently, as if on the brink of a finding. Then he puts the camera on a desk and a dialogue panel appears on the screen: *Get undressed!* She looks leery, but he points to the diplomas on the wall and she relents: *Oh well . . . if it's for science.* She unbuttons the dress and steps out of it, revealing an undershirt, a short slip. The dentist takes more pictures. Then he brings a small black music box down from a cupboard. He winds the spring, opens the cover, and places the box on a desk. A small ballerina turns slowly. Sandra shakes her head — *this dentist must be out of his mind!* — but even as she is thinking this, her body begins to move. The dentist takes his clothes off and joins her in an ardent dance. He lifts her over his head, lowers her lightly to the floor. She arches her long back and dashes around the examination room with her arms expressively behind her. This is Dr. Palomino's favorite part of the movie.

4 · Micah

WHAT A BIKE RIDER he was in his dreams. The front wheel spun true, minding his hands, and his chin floated high above the smooth turning of the pedals. Lyris appeared from nowhere, holding a jackknife with which to reward his new ability, but he did not want to stop long enough to take the prize. On and on, down the road, into town. Everyone had gathered along the sidewalks, but he glided past before they had time to cheer, and then the town lay behind him and the terrain changed. Mossy rocks loomed from the ditches, and the more they rose, the higher above the road he seemed to ride, until the bicycle had changed into an old-time model that had such a huge front wheel it would have to be mounted and dismounted with a ladder. He sped along, wondering how he would ever get down. A cold wind began to blow cotton snow that collected on the sleeves of his coat and on his eyelashes. Then the wheel began to shake, as it did when he was not dreaming. He looked for a place to bail out but was now riding over rough gray and green stones. The headwind drove furry scraps of snow against him. Weather slowed the bicycle, slowed the turns of the wheel, until finally, robbed of volition, the bicycle tilted toward the rocks and Micah fell and woke up on the floor of his bedroom.

He lay there breathing hard and listening to the night of the house. A familiar stream of sound came from downstairs. Everyone knew that television was a disruptive force that kept the mind from countless healthy activities such as reading and drawing, but still, how good it was to wake from a dream and hear a television playing. It meant his mother and father were still awake; sleep had not stolen them from him. Or, even if they were asleep, in front of the television screen, it was a still-dressed and slouching sleep, not nearly the dividing force presented by sleep in the bedroom. He was not allowed to enter their bedroom without knocking, and he assumed this rule had something to do with their dreams, which would be dramatic and complicated, and with "sexual intercourse," which would be too.

Micah opened Lyris's door far enough to slide into her room. The nightlight above the baseboard in the hallway cast a long thin el of light on the ceiling. It looked like the leg and foot of a thin man from the cartoons. Lyris breathed deeply and with a delicate vibration of the throat. An alarming gap fell between the completion of one breath and the beginning of the next. It might have been enough to make her faint if she had not already been unconscious. The sound of her breathing seemed to wrap Micah in its web. Moving to her dresser, he stepped on a rough cylinder with pearly inset buttons and knew it instantly for a corncob. Still his foot slipped and landed with a soft thud and he froze, waiting for her breath to resume. The top of her dresser yielded bobby pins, matches, a sandal, and a jewelry box. He wanted none of these things. He drifted back to the bed, where the reed of light crossed the night table and the sleeping Lyris. She was under the covers. One hand rimmed the base of her throat as if to protect it from the other, which lay on top of the blanket, upturned in a fist. As he had seen in the movies, Micah raised her arm and let it drop. He ran his fingernails lightly along the soft cords of her wrist; he pried open her fingers. He took the brushed-steel jackknife with the pheasant painting from her hand and backed to the doorway. Somewhere nearby a humidifier was running. Micah could just hear it beneath the sound of Lyris. He opened the knife and looked at the machined blade in the ray of light. He pressed the tip of the blade into his palm until it hurt. The knife closed soundlessly and tightly. It was an excellent knife. He put it back in Lyris's hand and closed her fingers.

Earl the deputy stopped by the tavern a couple hours into his nightly rounds. A sign on the wall said that the maximum number of people allowed on the premises was ninety-five, but there were only seven in the tavern, counting the bartender. "How's the old shillelagh?" he asked Earl.

"No complaints," said Earl. "Give me a Pepsi and a pickled egg."

The bartender uncapped a jar of brine and reached in with tongs. "I'm thinking of discontinuing these. We hardly sell any of them."

"Not like the old days," said the deputy, "when the pickled egg was king."

The bartender put the egg on a sheet of wax paper and handed it over. "Why, the sidewalks would be jammed with people, each with their own egg."

"That was the heyday of the steam-powered adding machine."

"Now everything's changed except the jokes."

"Old jokes for old men."

"All maintenance, here on out."

"How true."

Earl took the egg and the Pepsi to the back of the tavern and pressed coins into the metal sleeve of the pool table. The cast-resin balls rattled down the open shelf. He walked around the table, setting up trick shots. He ate the egg, which had the consistency of glue.

The young man named Follard came over and put quarters on the rail for a game of last-pocket. Follard shot from a crouch, peering over the edge of the table.

"You guys break up a party tonight?" he said.

"Not me."

"Then who would it have been?"

Earl shrugged and sank a bank shot he had no business making.

"Well, I heard some kids got their keg taken from a party at the Elephant."

"Entirely possible, but it's nothing I've heard of," said Earl. "And these were cops that did it?"

"So it was told to me," said Follard.

Earl took a five-dollar bill from his shirt pocket and folded it into a sleeve, which he slid down the cue, ferrule to joint. "What am I again?"

"Little ones."

"I can't even remember what I am. That's where my head is at."

"I got a knife off them."

"Off who?"

"The ones who told me about the party."

"They just offered it up. Out of generosity."

"Out of something. They don't know where it went."

"Well, Follard, what'd you take it for? You see, this is how you get in trouble."

Follard reached under the table for the bridge.

"The ladies' aid," commented Earl.

Follard held the butt of the bridge in one hand and fitted the cue intently into the brass notch. "To tell you the truth, I don't even know why I did it."

"Don't think I won't run you in."

"For a little jackknife? Put it this way: it would surprise me."

"Let me see it."

"I gave it to a girl."

Earl folded his arms with the cue against his badge. "I ought to rough you up or something."

"Why do you say that?"

"I don't know. It's just a feeling. Like it would be an ounce of prevention."

"Well, she's more deserving than the one who lost it. In a sense, I did a good thing."

"I highly doubt it," said Earl.

Micah crept down the stairs. Because of how the house was built, you could get two thirds of the way without being seen. His father sat in the big chair, and his mother was on the davenport with her legs crossed beneath her. They were watching a movie on Channel 9. The commercials were bracketed with film footage of clouds passing eerily over the moon, followed by the words *Nightcap Theater,* written in letters that were drawn to look as if they were made of wooden planks, jagged from hasty breaking. Charles yawned and opened a bottle of beer, and Joan flipped through a stack of index cards on which she had written notes for the speech she would give over the weekend in the city. Micah scratched the center of his back with his thumb. His back always itched. When he observed his parents together and they were not aware of being watched, he thought of them by their names. Joan's talk was about giving more freedom to the dogs and cats in shelters. That way not only would the animals have a more interesting life, she said, but the visitors who might adopt them would get a stronger sense of their personalities than if they saw them in cages, where they could only slink.

"I just thought of something," said Joan. "What if they're already doing these things? Maybe I'll be preaching to the converted."

Charles shrugged. "I find that unlikely," he said. "And even if you are telling them what they want to hear, so what? They still want to hear it."

"It all sounds so obvious."

"You've read it six times, that's why."

"Maybe I should cut this part about scratching posts."

"Dance with the one who brung you, I say."

"I'd give anything just to stay home."

"No, you wouldn't."

"Yes, I would."

"You can't wait."

"I couldn't stay home if I wanted to. I've made commitments. You work alone. No one decides what you're going to do except you."

"You can't wait to get in the water."

"I must take direction," said Joan. "What do you mean by that?"

"Who directed you to pack a swimming suit?"

"I'm going to a hotel. There may be a pool. Therefore, I'm taking a swimming suit."

"You meet someone, you have a nice swim, you towel off."

Joan took a deep breath and squared up her index cards. "Why did your first marriage end?"

Charles held his beer bottle up to the light and looked at it. "Many reasons."

"Jealousy."

"That was one of them."

"That was a big one of them. This feeling you have of, of, of *ownership*."

"Oh, hell."

Joan sighed. "But let's don't start."

"Good."

"Let's change the subject." She looked around the living room. "There was a man in the yard tonight."

"Who?"

"Someone with a metal detector, according to Lyris. I didn't like the sound of it."

"Don't tell him," said Micah, before he realized that he was not supposed to be there.

"Micah?" said Joan. "What are you doing up?"

"Don't tell me what?" Charles said.

"I can't sleep."

"Come on down, honey," said Joan.

"What shouldn't she tell me?"

Micah sat beside Joan on the davenport and told Charles how he had shut Lyris in the barn.

"What is with you?" said Charles. "Think what would happen if you couldn't get it unlocked."

"She would break the doors."

"You hope she would."

"No," said Joan. "She did."

"Lyris broke the doors of the barn?"

"With a shovel," said Micah.

"No kidding. Lyris is a tough one. But don't ever try that again."

"Are you mad?"

"I don't want her locked in the barn. Everything is broken around here, and I don't expect the barn doors will make any difference."

"Can we still get a goat?" said Micah.

"We'll see."

The movie came on again. Charlie Chaplin was in a tavern with a pretty woman. They were dancing. Charlie had belted his pants with a rope, and the rope was tied to a dog. Then a cat showed up and the dog leaped after it, causing Charlie Chaplin to spill to the ground.

"Isn't Chaplin the greatest?" said Joan. "I'll bet he is the finest actor who ever lived."

"What about Tommy Lee Jones and Sissy Spacek in that coal-mining movie?" said Charles.

"Apples and oranges," said Joan.

"That was a damned good film."

Joan returned to her index cards.

"I *like* that scratching post part," said Micah.

Joan smiled, and her eyes flickered like the dark part of fire. "You hear everything, don't you?"

Charles sat forward in the big chair and tightened the laces of his boots with strong tugs. "I'm going to go see about the barn."

The three got up and went out through the kitchen. Joan lifted the green dress and folded it over her arm. Micah slid his bare feet into sneakers. In the boot room, they took coats from pegs.

The clouds had gone. Micah looked for the hunter in the constellation Orion, but all he could see was an enormous piece of bow-tie pasta. He was hungry. Sometimes his mother read to him from the Audubon book of the night sky. Once she told how Artemis, huntress and moon goddess, had shot Orion with an arrow, thinking he was someone else. To make amends, she placed his body in the sky, with his dogs for company. *This is why the moon has been cold and empty ever since,* said his mother, shaking her head. *This is why.* She began to read again; Orion got his strength back by chasing the nymphs of Taurus. It was unclear to Micah whether his mother regarded this as a suitable ending. But he wished all these things were really happening in the sky.

Charles shined a flashlight on the broken wood and hanging

sp. "How do you expect to have a goat when this is what ou do to a door?"

The comparison seemed wrong to Micah. "Nobody would hurt a goat."

Charles sighed. "Oh, I don't suppose you would on purpose."

Joan took the flashlight and the dress into the barn. "No goats until you fix these doors," she said.

"I don't know how."

Joan came out, clapping her hands free of dust. "Maybe not," she said, "but it won't get you out of helping."

"That's fair," said Micah.

Charles pushed the doors shut and secured them with a cement block. He was always rearranging the pieces that had worked loose from the foundation.

The light of the moon made a black shadow at the base of the hedge. You could hide there and no one would know until sunrise. Micah looked at the stained face of the moon. Men had gone up there years ago but found nothing worthwhile. It was all a pointless exercise, Charles had said. One of the things that he did best was to discover the pointlessness of exercises. He would scan the newspaper for useless behavior. Joan, however, would always try to see the reason behind what she read. She took everything to heart and would focus on stories of murder and abduction. Joan and Charles seemed like opposites, and Micah could not understand how they had ever got together. In fairy tales, the man and the woman were sometimes assigned to each other by cruel parents, but this did not happen anymore. Joan once told him how she had met Charles at a lecture on alcohol in a church. Later they lived in the church. Imagine living in a church! Alcohol was one of the four menaces lying in wait for the unsuspecting child: alcohol, drugs, television, and cigarettes. The cigarettes seemed worst to Micah, because your lungs turned black, and you died, and warts could grow out of your eyebrows, as had happened in the case of a worker at the grain elevator. Micah was glad that Charles and Joan did not smoke cigarettes or take drugs, although they did drink alcohol. And of course they all watched television, on which men and women smoked and drank and undercover policemen laid out on tables the drugs they had seized. The drugs came in packages of white paper, like pork chops.

As the three were walking back to the house, a shooting star crossed the sky. They stood looking at the nothing that was left of it. Micah wished that warts would not grow from his eyebrows if he ever took up smoking. What his parents wished for, he could not guess. Then, as if they had been waiting for it, they heard the sound of a window opening.

"Is someone there?" said Lyris.

She leaned out the window, with her hands on the shingles over the boot room.

"Hello?"

Why was no one answering? Micah wondered. It was true that they were all on the shy side in her presence. Charles would sometimes look at Lyris and set his jaw, as if trying to think of something to say. Then he would hurry off — past her or away from her. Joan spoke to Lyris as if she were hard of hearing or very young. And Micah called her sister, not only because Joan thought it would help reinforce their relationship but also as a way of papering over the fact that she was nearly a stranger to him.

"Just us, Lyris," said Joan. "Mother and Dad and Micah. We came out to see about the barn doors."

Lyris climbed out the window and stood on the roof. *We don't know her,* thought Micah, *and she doesn't know us.* She steadied her hand on the window frame and said she was sorry.

"I don't blame you," said Charles. "Nobody wants to be locked inside something."

"It's my fault," said Micah.

"It's Micah's fault," said Charles.

"But don't be coming out on the roof," said Joan. "You could fall, Lyris. That's no place for a young woman."

"Maybe we could meet up somewhere in the house and continue this discussion," said Charles.

Lyris climbed back through the window and slid it closed. A police car rolled slowly by, spotlight angling this way and that, picking out fence posts and black trees and the silver mailbox before coming to rest on Charles, Joan, and Micah. The car backed up, wheeled into the driveway, and the big cop Earl Kellogg got out.

"You folks're up late. Everything all right?"

"You've got no work here," said Charles. "Micah couldn't sleep, so we came out to look at the barn."

"That always works when I'm feeling sleepless."

"The kids broke the doors."

"Well, I heard you had an extra one lately."

"Lyris came this summer," said Joan.

"Mind if I see her? Just for the sake of the thing."

"Come on in," said Charles.

Earl followed them into the house, holster flexing with a leathery sound.

"Lyris," called Joan. "Oh, look at what time it's getting to be. I have to get up in five hours."

Lyris came downstairs in a white robe with red threads.

"This is Earl," said Joan. "He's with the sheriff's department. We've known him forever."

"Seems like it, anyhow." Earl smiled and shook Lyris's hand. "Welcome to Grouse County."

"He happened by while we were all standing out in the yard like geese," said Joan, "so he wanted to check in and say hello."

"Hello," said Lyris.

Earl turned to Charles. "You wouldn't have any beer, would you?"

"You came to our school and said not to drink and drive," Micah said.

"And don't forget it. But somehow a glass of keg beer would go real well 'long about now. What do you say, Tiny?"

Joan looked from one man to the other and pointed out that everyone called her husband Charles now.

"What do you say about that, Charles?"

"We've got bottled beer, but I can't offer you a draw. Tell you what I will do, however. I'll ask you to get out of here and find your own beer."

Earl laughed, but his heart was not in it. "So that's how you'd have it. The truth is, I haven't drunk a beer in ages. If anything, I might have a spot of vodka. But only after a meal and never behind the wheel, as they say."

"I'm going to bed," said Lyris.

"Me too," said Joan. "Come on, Micah. Time for all good children to be dreaming in their beds."

"I hope you like our part of the country, Lyris," said Earl. "And if you ever want to stop by the sheriff's office and see the inner workings of justice, just give a holler."

"Thank you, I might."

Earl left, Joan turned off the lights, and they all went up to bed. Micah set himself the task of planning for the arrival of the goat. They would drive fence posts and rig a wire fence. Micah and Lyris could feed and brush it, shine its hooves with cloth, and show it at the fair. They would need buckets for the oats, or whatever it would eat, and buckets appealed to him. Metal ones. He fell asleep hearing the clanking of the handles.

❧ Saturday

5 · Lyris

LYRIS WOKE in the morning and found Follard's jack-knife under the pillow. She considered cutting Micah's shoestrings with it, but what kind of revenge would that be? He could just get new ones. She turned onto her back in the sagging bed. The mattress rested on what appeared from underneath to be a panel of hog fence. No matter which end she placed her head at, her feet were higher. When she slept on her side, the bed put such a twist in her spine that she felt old and bent the next day.

But wasn't that the way? she thought. The cracks in the ceiling reminded her of the Great Lakes. *Homes* was the word that helped you remember their names. Until you were on your own, you took the makeshift bed given you and dreamed of the strong beautiful bed you would have for yourself some-day. She got dressed and went downstairs. Light filled the kitchen. She smelled pancakes and the dusty husks of the corn-field across the road. Soon the corn would be harvested and bound for the river in semitrailer trucks and hopper cars. Charles had explained this.

She stood in the doorway, waiting for her life to come back to her body. Saturdays here seemed aimless, windblown, whereas in the orphanage they had been days of cleaning. All the kids would walk around with mops in their hands and the sting of bleach in their noses.

Charles slid three pancakes from a spatula onto Lyris's plate. "What's this about someone with a metal detector in the yard last night?"

"He said his name was Follard and he was lost," said Lyris. She uncapped a bottle of clear corn syrup, which looked like furniture polish.

Charles sat in a chair backward, the rounded rail under his arms. The sleeves of his blue sweatshirt were cut above the elbows. "Did you ask him over?"

Lyris cut her pancakes with knife and fork, wondering what Charles was trying to be. He was a mystery. A shadow moved across his eyes. "No sir. I've never seen him before. He just walked up out of the grove." Charles's hair was thick and black — Micah said he dyed it — and a bit shaggy where it curled over his ears.

"He's no one you want to know," said Charles. "The best you can do with a kid like that is stay away."

Someone, she suspected, had said the same about Charles one time or another. She could see in his face that when talking about Follard, he was talking about himself as well. That's how he could be so sure.

"Did Mom leave already?"

"Yes, about three hours before she had to. But understand what I say about Follard. And if he comes around again when Joan and I aren't here, I want you to tell him whose place this is. I'll tell him if he doesn't get it. And we don't want any metal detecting on our land."

"All right. I understand."

"Maybe he's got the idea that whatever's under the ground is free for the taking. This is not how it works."

"No."

"I know this kind of kid. And I say it for your own good and believing full well that you can take care of yourself."

"Which I will."

The dead and seedless head of a sunflower moved across a windowpane. Charles's eyes met hers and did not look away. "Can I ask how you got your name?"

"Well, there was a garden at the orphanage, and the gardener, not the one they had when I was there but some other one before that, her name was Lyris."

"And later, when you had foster parents —"

She ate a wedge of pancakes from the flat of her knife while waiting for him to go on.

"Which were the ones that made bombs?"

"Pete and Jackie. But I don't know if they really made them. They had the instructions and all."

"And none of them ever wanted to change your name."

Lyris thought for a moment. "Why? Do you think I should?"

"No. It's a nice name and it suits you. I just wanted to know how it works, with the foster parents and everything. Joan got Micah's name out of the Bible."

"I thought she might have," said Lyris. "What did this Follard ever do?"

"They say he burned his parents' house. I don't know the whole story. I didn't really follow it. It happened some years ago. He went to court, but they couldn't prove what happened."

"Did he really?"

"Who knows? They say he did."

"I think he might have been lost, like he said."

Charles got up from the chair. "This is not an easy place to get lost in."

"All right."

"Can I make you more pancakes?"

"No, thank you."

"There's a special one you better have."

He carried her plate to the stove and came back with a scrap of browned batter in the shape of a cursive L. "That's for Lyris," he said.

After breakfast they drove over to Charles's brother's place to build new doors for the barn. Jerry had a table saw and a lumber pile. In his faded blue postal clothes and the white pith helmet that shaded his eyes, he sat on the front steps by a silver keg, drinking a glass of beer. Charles sorted through the lumber, measuring boards with a tape. He dragged out the ones he wanted and put them on the wet grass in the sun. The boards were of different colors, but weathered and faded so that the same grayness of grain showed through all of them.

Jerry came down the steps and stood by the wood. "Caught me on my break."

"You know," said Charles, "a policeman came by our place looking for a keg last night."

"Same here."

"What'd you say?"

"Not much I could say with the evidence so evident. But you know Earl. He's more curious to know what happened than he is eager to put himself out. He did say he would get my lights taken away if I misused them."

"He must have come over here after being at our place."

"I imagine, but he didn't say so."

"Always one step ahead, isn't he?"

"Not hardly. What are you making?"

"Barn doors."

Jerry got into his car and drove off to deliver the mail, leaving the three of them in the lonely blue light of his place down in the hollow. They worked all morning, and it never seemed to get any later. Lyris and Micah brought out sawhorses from a corrugated metal building. Charles tried to be patient with Jerry's warped lumber, but he swore and raked his fingers and misplaced his tools. Watching him trying to contain his unruly nature was like watching someone tie himself up with rope. Lyris and Micah liked it when he lost his tools, because then they could pick them up and hand them to him. Charles ran the circular saw while Micah and Lyris helped steady the boards on the sawhorses. Sawdust flew in furry arcs that coated their arms and necks. Charles went out of his way to show them the way that things should be done, demonstrating how the release of the thumb lock made the steel tape race back into its housing, and how when a frame was square, the measurements on the diagonal were exactly the same. When the measurements differed, though, he seemed uncertain what to do about it. Lyris chewed the skin on the side of a fingernail, thinking that big things they had no clue about were happening somewhere else in the world.

Eventually they got the planks sawed and laid out over backing frames with X-shaped crosspieces to keep them "on the square." Then it was time to nail, which came as a relief, because they could all take equal part, slugging away, with little precision required. Planks gapped in places, and the ends were not always even, but Charles said they could caulk the gaps and saw the ends back at home, where he had a chalk line somewhere. Each door was too heavy for all three of them to lift, but somehow not too heavy for Charles alone to lift. He put them into the back of his pickup, and they rode home, where they tore down the old doors and set about hanging the new ones. Charles screwed the straps of the old hinges into place. The doors opened and closed better than Lyris expected, and looked all right, except that one door was green, the other blue and red. That could be fixed with the painting, which would wait for another day.

* * *

In the afternoon they went to an auction house called the Palace to find a goat for sale. This was a big square building of whitewashed brick flanked on either side by open-sided sheds and alleys of matted straw. Cows lowed in the sheds, and Micah ran toward the noise. He stopped short, however, before a large circle of dark and shining blood on the straw. When Lyris and Charles caught up, they discussed what might have occasioned the spilling of the blood and why it had happened right here, but none of them could get a mental picture of the violence.

"My uncle one time got a calf to raise and slaughter," said Charles. "He was going to make himself into a gentleman farmer. He'd read all about it, but it wasn't in him, you know? The seasons passed, and the calf got bigger, and when it came time to kill the thing, he couldn't do it. They had that cow until it died of old age. It would follow my uncle around and come when called. When it died, they dug a big hole out back of the house and buried it there."

"Appalling," said Lyris.

They walked down the aisle between the pens. The cows moved slowly, as if embarrassed about their great size. The hogs lay splayed out on their sides, oblivious.

"They look hot," said Lyris.

"A pig will look hot in any weather," said Charles. "They're just hot-looking."

"Where are the goats?" said Micah.

"I'm wondering the same."

Flies buzzed the blinking eyes of a pink sow with black spots. "What if God is some kind of livestock?" said Lyris. "People will have a lot of explaining to do."

"They have that no matter what God is," said Charles.

"Or a lobster," said Micah. "How would you like to be a lobster and get boiled alive in a big pot?"

"I wouldn't go for that," said Charles.

"I seen it on TV."

"Alive? Hard to believe."

"Oh, it's true," said Lyris.

"What do you eat of a lobster, anyway?" said Charles. "Doesn't seem like there'd be a lot of meat on them."

"They're crustaceans," said Micah.

"Well, I wouldn't eat a lobster if you paid me," said Charles. "And I wouldn't eat rabbit, although many do."

"There's a goat," said Micah. He was looking into someone's yard, where an animal slept in the grass beneath a tree.

"Hell, that's a dog," said Charles.

Lyris smiled as she followed Charles and Micah into the main building. There was something she liked about Charles, although he knew so little about lobsters.

The three of them walked up a set of wide and uneven stairs and came out at the top of an old wooden auditorium, semicircular in design. The bleachers descended steeply, in ever tighter arcs, to a dirt pen two or three stories below.

"Imagine building this," said Charles. "We had trouble with them simple doors."

The bleachers were half full of farmers. Some talked, some smoked, some held radios to their ears. They wore widelegged pinstriped overalls and cloth hats crushed down on their heads. The auctioneer stood at a raised platform at the back of the pen. The wall above his head had hand-painted signs for feed companies, well drillers, implement dealers, veterinarians, and banks. The biggest sign of all was a disclaimer: ALL GUARANTEES ARE BETWEEN THE BUYER AND THE SELLER WITH NONE MADE BY THE AUCTIONEER. Lyris felt she'd happened on some ancient place.

They walked down an aisle and took seats as the next sale was beginning. A door opened beside the auctioneer's stand and five hogs sauntered into the pen, ringed noses testing the air. They were followed by a man slapping a wooden slat against his thigh and calling, "Suh! Suh!" He wore knee-high boots of black rubber with terra-cotta soles. Lyris expected the auctioneer's speech to be hypnotic, nonstop, and indecipherable; she was ready for a torrent. Instead he said calmly, in a drawl more occupational than regional, that these were American Landrace barrows certified by the seller free of cholera and Bang's disease and mange.

After the hogs were sold, the man with the flat stick and high boots bowed to the bleachers and herded the animals back through the doorway in the wall. Charles asked a group of farmers sitting below them when the goats were expected to go on the block, or had they already gone?

The farmers laughed. An old man wearing round eyeglasses asked what Charles had said. When it was repeated to him, the old man craned his neck to see who had asked such a thing. "Why, the goddamned dummy," he said.

"Saturdays are hogs and cattle only," explained another farmer. Using a blunt-nosed pencil, he was writing figures on a scrap of brown paper.

Charles gave the old farmer a wary glance. "What day are the goats?"

"They don't get a day," said the writing farmer. "It's not an auction animal. Not that I know of, anyway." He turned away. "Skel! This fellow wants to know about goats."

Skel stood up and looked around. "We haven't had a goat, geez, going on ten years."

"Let's go, Daddy," said Micah.

"There's no money in it," said Skel. "I can tell you from sad experience, you're better off with cattle."

"Let's go."

"You're telling me they don't auction goats," said Charles, hemmed in, it seemed, by everything they knew and he didn't. "That it isn't done."

It wasn't really clear whom he was talking to, but the farmer with the scrap of paper folded it and put it in the pocket of his green down vest. "I wouldn't go that far," he said. "I could believe it happens somewhere."

"They don't auction goats in this county!" said the old man, as if the county's honor had been called into question.

"They're more suited to hill country," said Skel. "You've come to the wrong place, son."

Charles lifted his chin proudly, surveying the farmers arrayed against him. "Watch me," he said. He got up and walked down the aisle to the pen, where he pushed open a gate and strode through. He stepped onto the platform and addressed the auctioneer, who listened impassively, as auctioneers will.

"Who is he, anyway?" someone asked.

"Our father," said Lyris.

The old man with the round glasses opened a flat tin and offered it to Micah. "Want a Sucret?" he said.

A rowdy calf was sold, kicking and snorting, and then another pack of hogs. Charles reappeared from above and took a seat beside Lyris.

"I don't mind, Dad," she said.

"When you bid," he said quietly, "just raise your hand."

The next animal for sale was a white cow, which no one bid on, and it was withdrawn. Then the man with the flat stick pushed the door open and dragged in a goat by a rope looped around its neck. It had a shaggy reddish coat that reached nearly to the ground. Once it saw the audience, it moved ahead of the man, strolling in a stately manner around the pen, like a float in a parade.

"This is a Toggenburg doe, two years of age," said the auctioneer. "I'm looking for a bid of sixty-five dollars."

Charles nudged Lyris, who raised her hand.

"Sold," said the auctioneer. "Young woman in the seventh row's got herself a goat."

Lyris felt all the eyes in the auction house on her. Maybe that was an exaggeration. But she had not felt chosen in this way since the Home Bringers stole her from her ironing board.

At a feed store on the way home they bought forty pounds of alfalfa pellets, a leather collar, and two metal pans. Charles pounded a stake into the back yard and tied the goat to it, leaving enough slack for her to get under the porch roof in case of rain. The goat's eyes were slotted and lively, and she smelled like hot hay. Lyris set out a pan of water and another pan of the dark green alfalfa pellets. The goat showed no interest. Then Micah carried a lawn chair over next to the goat and sat down. This was a mistake. The goat butted the chair over, and Micah ran off. The goat walked over the chair with some difficulty. Charles cuffed her on her bony forehead and told her to cut it out, and she butted him. Then all three of them stood beyond the reach of the rope and watched the goat lower her head to the pan of water.

"How did you know they had a goat?" said Lyris.

Charles smiled. "I know the auctioneer. I called him last night, set the whole thing up."

"But then," said Lyris, "why did you ask those men?"

"Because I knew what they would say."

There was a home football game that night, and the older 4-H girls went over to the field together in a club van. They would run the concession stand and earn the proceeds. The rival football players got off buses and stood around holding their helmets against their hips and blinking at the falling sun, their heads looking small and innocent above the platelike shoulder pads. It seemed to Lyris that any sport requiring so much padding had yet to arrive at an appropriate set of rules.

The game started. The fans prowled the sidelines with leather flasks and thermoses, screaming for progress. The band members stood in goofy uniforms, playing their instruments, and occasionally one would take off after sheet music that had escaped its harp-shaped holder to skip over the ground in the fall wind. It was an absurd and lovely spectacle for someone raised in an orphanage and by suburban terrorists. On break from the concession stand, Lyris stood behind the end zone, watching the roving street brawl of the game and drinking hot chocolate with Octavia Perry and two other girls from 4-H. Suddenly Octavia was being nice to her, and what a blessing this kindness seemed, if somewhat sinister.

"Isn't this good cocoa?" said Octavia. "It's so, like, chocolatey I could drink a barrel of the shit."

"You've put something in it, haven't you?" said Lyris.

Octavia smiled at her. She had blazing dark eyes and coral beads in her hair. "It's possible."

"Oh, drink up, Lyris," said a thin girl named Mercedes Wonsmos. "You don't have to be so Christlike all the time. Don't try to iron us the way you iron your slacks."

"Yeah, you can drop that tiresome act," said Echo Anderson. "We've decided to be your friends, but you have to be genuine with us."

"I have been. I'm not Christlike."

"Have some cocoa," said Octavia.

The crowd started yelling. The wave of sound rose and rolled their way. A small boy from the home team staggered into the end zone with the ball in his arms and a tall, thick-bodied opposing boy holding on to his leg.

"I scored! Let go! I'm going to spike!"

"I say you ain't," said the larger boy.

The referee raised his arms as if someone had pulled a gun on him and then tugged the fighting boys apart.

A squad of cheerleaders sprinted down the field with fists pressed awkwardly to their sides. "Ahhh, cut me some slack, 'cause if you don't, I won't, scratch your back," they shouted.

The 4-H girls looked at each other and shook their heads in

the steam rising from their cups. "I don't know why we even have to drink when life itself is so fascinating," said Mercedes Wonsmos.

The sarcastic delivery of her remark did not make it false. Lyris liked the cold hilltop field and the high lonely banks of floodlights and the white jerseys of the home team and the field so bright and the sky so dark. She took the pieces of the night into her heart and had room for more, as if her heart were as big as the auction house. Now the boy who had scored the touchdown spun free of the gyrating cheerleaders and came so near that she could have counted the cat decals on his dull gold helmet. He had an eager, what-next expression on his face and reminded her of Micah. She put her foot out and tripped him, settling a score that he could not have been aware of. Down he went on the grass, but he bounced up immediately, as if his fall were intended, a new part of the scoring ritual. His teammates gathered around, slapping and punching him to convey their approval. All of their helmets had the cat stickers, given for accomplishments on the field. The team seemed rich in achievement indeed, though it had yet to win a game. But this illusion was all right too, beautiful in its way, for if they counted themselves better than they were, then couldn't she do the same? "Go, Fighting Cats," she found herself crying, "go," as if urging the boys to leave the field and the town and strike out through the bristling dry cornfields for the perilous journey to adulthood. Yes, she was thoroughly drunk, but with some clarity of vision, and at this moment she turned to see Follard standing among the thick and curving pipes of the pumping station behind the field. He saw her too. He swung down from the bolted blue jungle and came to the field's end.

"I'm carrying your knife," she said.

"Give it to me."

6 · Charles

WHEN IT GOT LATE and Lyris didn't come home, Charles left her a note explaining that he had been called out on a job and had taken Micah with him. He went to the boot room and unlocked a cabinet, from which he took the double-barreled Savage shotgun that, of his three long-barreled guns, most resembled the one held so dear by Farina Matthews. Outside, he opened the door of the pickup and exchanged the gun for the umbrella he kept as a joke in the gun rack. He leaned the umbrella on the porch and went upstairs and into Micah's room. The boy had fallen asleep in his clothes.

"Wake up," said Charles. "Wake up. You're going on a sleepover."

They drove down the road with the moon cruising lopsided and bright over the town and bridges and fields. Micah slept with an Indian blanket on his legs, his head nodding against the passenger window of the truck. Charles carried him crosswise into his mother's house, put him on the davenport, and settled the blanket over him. In sleep, the boy's innocence seemed so absolute that it was hard for Charles to imagine it would not last forever.

In the kitchen, wondering where Colette might be, he saw two black speakers in metal casings on the counter and heard a scrabbling noise coming from the cracked linoleum at his feet. As he watched, a double-stranded wire emerged from a small hole in the floor, frazzled ends extended.

"Mom?" he called.

"I'm in the cellar" came her muffled reply.

He went out behind the house and ducked under a clothesline hung with stiff worn dresses swaying in the wind. The bulkhead doors lay open, spilling pale light on the grass. Charles's mother was coming slowly up the stairs with wire cutters and electrical tape.

"I wonder if you could help me," said Charles.

"I wonder if I could." She stopped on the steps to turn off the light. "What time is it?"

"Eleven-thirty. I got called out on a job, but I'm watching Micah."

Colette handed up the tape and the cutters. "Joan told me she was going away."

"When'd you see Joan?"

"She came by yesterday, wanting me to ask Farina Matthews for that gun you like."

"She knows my mind," said Charles.

"What good would it do?"

"Probably none," Charles agreed. "I've tried talking to Farina, but I get nowhere."

"What do you want with it?"

"More than she does, I would think."

"It didn't belong to your father anyway. It belonged to your sister Bebe's father."

"I know."

Colette pulled clothespins from the hanging wash and laid the dresses over Charles's arms. "Say you got it. So what?" she said. She led the way into the house, where Charles dropped the clothes into a wooden basket with broken slats.

"Now if you'll be so kind as to fetch up those wires," she said.

"Micah's in the living room." When he lifted the guillotine catches of the speakers and secured the wires, music began to play. It sounded like the wailing and mourning of many men.

"What are we listening to?"

"This is the Hilliard Ensemble, singing the 'Mass for Four Voices' by Thomas Tallis," said Colette. She picked up a CD case from the top of the stove and took out the accompanying booklet and read. "'It is not possible for a man to rise above himself and his humanity,' says Montaigne. 'We are, I know not how, double in ourselves, so that what we believe we disbelieve, and cannot rid ourselves of what we condemn.' What do you think? Agree? Disagree?"

The voices faded to silence and then began again. He pictured the singers climbing a steep rock, on top of which waited some fate that they were afraid of but that they had to face or they would never feel right. "It does hit home."

"Doesn't it?"

"Who's Montaigne?"

"Some thinker of great degree, from the sound of it."

"I'm going."

"What happened, someone's pipes give out?"

"No one you know."

"If it's true, I believe you," said Colette.

They went to look at Micah, who slept with his face resting on hands that were pressed together in the attitude of prayer.

Charles left the house and closed the door, but he could still hear the voices of the Hilliard Ensemble. He took the roundabout route toward Grafton, where Farina Matthews lived, and plunged his truck down a lane between two cornfields.

Then he parked, put his feet up on the seat and his back against the door, drank some whiskey and Coke from a Mason jar, and went to sleep. When he woke, he looked at his watch and took the gun from the rack behind the seat and walked through a field with the sound of leaves rustling in his ears. Some odd hunter he made in the black trough of the nighttime cornrow.

When the field ended, he climbed the fence and walked across the quiet yards of the town. On the back side of the widow's house, he leaned the shotgun against the clapboard, slit the screen above the weatherboard with a utility knife, and separated the hook from the eye that secured the screen. He rested the screen against the house, raised the sash, and went in, first one leg, then his torso, and then the other leg, not forgetting the shotgun, which he held in one hand, bringing it sideways through the open window. Mrs. Matthews's black Labrador came padding and panting into the room. He scratched the dog on the back of the neck. It collapsed, melted to the floor, turned on its side. Charles stood up and looked around. It had been a long time since he had stolen something, but he had no trouble finding the old thrill of it. In the wrong house, at the wrong time, he felt alive. But this wasn't stealing, anyway; it was more like trading.

In her bed, Farina Matthews dreamed in that familiar mode in which something that happened long ago is happening again, except with new fantastic touches that constitute the dream's imaginary or psychological aspect. She knew it was a dream while having it; it was lucid dreaming. She and the Reverend Matthews were driving along in their Edsel with the deep seats and pushbutton transmission, a car ahead of its time, although the dream reconstructed an incident from so long ago that by now both the car's actual time and the time it had been ahead of had well passed. They were going up to the hospital, where he would visit sick parishioners and she would distribute gifts to the new mothers. In those days hospitals did not hustle the women out the door as they do now but kept them languishing for days. The bewildered and isolated mothers were always happy to receive a basket of soaps and blankets and pacifiers, tied with ribbon. In the dream, however, the baskets were full of the kitchen rags from beneath Mrs. Matthews's sink.

On the way to the hospital they encountered a hitchhiker, and the reverend pulled over. An open trailer was hooked to the car, and she saw the man walking up past its wooden side. He had short hair and melancholy eyes and was dressed like a laborer. His name was Sandover. He was Charles's stepfather.

"Afternoon," said the reverend. "Where you headed?"

"Morrisville."

"Get in. What did you put in the trailer?" Farina's husband was always so observant. He could see rain on the horizon of what looked to anyone else like a clear day.

"A shotgun."

"What are you going to do in Morrisville?"

"Well, I'll tell you. I got laid off at the molasses plant, and I heard they might be planning to call some back."

"With the gun, though."

"The gun I hope to register at a pawnshop."

The reverend drove along for a while, then said, "I'll give you forty for it."

"This is unexpected."

"I'll give you sixty dollars and you can leave it right there in the trailer and save yourself going to the pawnshop."

"The thing is, I'll want it back when the work starts up again and I can redeem the price."

"That's a promise."

"It's a good gun. It's light and it looks smart and it hardly kicks at all. And I think you'll find that it shoots accurate. But I should tell you it's a four-ten. It's not really a beginner's gun, although many consider it to be one, without thinking it through. Maybe you don't want to hear about this."

"No, it's fascinating."

"Well, some are of the opinion that you give a small-bore gun to a kid who's just starting off in their shooting. The problem is they won't be able to hit anything with it, and whatever they do hit, they might just wing, so that it gets down in the brush and runs, or drags along till it meets up with a fox or a hawk. Not that you want something too massive. A twenty-gauge isn't a bad idea. But the four-ten is more of a gun for the specialist."

The reverend did not like to have anyone alter the position of his rearview mirror, so Farina turned to look at the back seat. Jack Sandover had opened one of the baskets and draped the rags up and down his arms. Now her son was in the back seat too, not grown, but still a child. "Stop the car," her boy said. "At the rate we're going, I'll never get my doctorate."

Farina's husband pulled over on the shoulder and they all got out to look in the trailer. The shotgun rested on a bed of straw. Sandover picked it up and began dismantling it, handing out the pieces of wood and metal. Then the car began moving, with the child behind the wheel. Farina ran after the car, dropping shotgun parts on the pavement while Sandover laughed. The steering wheel emerged from the window, for it had come off in the boy's hand. The Edsel veered from one side of the highway to the other, and thick black smoke rolled from the chassis.

The dream had turned ominous, and Farina woke herself by force of will. She got up and went to the bathroom for a drink of water. Waves of guilt seemed to travel down her back; what sort of guilt? she wondered. She looked in the mirror, noting sleep's contradictory effects. It made her look older but feel younger, with all the fears and anxieties of a young woman, uncertain of herself and what life would bring. Yet she told herself to wake up, because most of what life would bring had already arrived. She had her health and her income and her collection of miniature lighthouses, which seemed an ironic commentary on her never having seen a real one. Once there had been a fake lighthouse at a restaurant on the lake. Even here, in the middle of so much land, everyone thought of the sea, as if in genetic recollection of the Flood, looking out from the island of Ararat with perhaps a cardinal bird on each shoulder, the red male and the fawn female, if cardinals lived in that faraway place.

She drained the water glass and the dream came back to her in fragments — the rags on the man's arms, the crumbling gun, the sunlight sliding like oil over the Edsel's lavender hood. She did not know why the night had to be so heartbreaking, unless its simple loneliness served as an intimation of the final solitude. But she was not alone, or at least something unusual was going on. She heard the rapid thump of the dog's leg, its involuntary scratching, and she heard intermittent footfalls followed by long silences, as if someone were stepping on stones in a pool of water that rose to reclaim each rock once it had been disturbed, and she heard random small metallic clicks and scrapes that seemed to underscore the material nature of our lives. She had laughed last spring, reading of the high school's plan for a substance-free prom. She had imagined the disembodied seniors floating like wandering souls in a bottomless miasmal gymnasium.

Farina could not defend herself without a weapon, so she went to the closet and selected a cedar clothes hanger that was good stout wood on all three sides, with the image of an evergreen burned into its apex, below the hook. She moved silently, while conceding to herself that the correct approach might be to turn on the lights and make all kinds of noise. On the other hand, if the intruder were after her and not her television set or the good silver that came from Rainy Lake, then creating a racket would only be playing a high card to his inevitable trump. It surprised her how calm she felt. She did not want to lose the Rainy Lake silver, which was packed in a zippered burgundy case so well made that the forks could only be wrenched from their felt slots.

"Take the television," she whispered. "Take the television and go."

Charles lifted his stepfather's shotgun from the rack on which it rested and broke open the barrels to make sure no shells were inside. He laid the gun on the davenport before putting the other one in its place. Then he heard Mrs. Matthews moving slowly down the stairs. He could not get the shotgun and himself out the window before her arrival, so he sat down in a chair to wait for her. Best not to go running around, because a house with one gun may well have two. More shootings occur in mutual panic and confusion than when one of the parties is sitting in a chair. He might even turn on a light; yes, that would be a good idea. There was a lamp on a table next to the chair. It had one of those elusive cord switches, and as he groped up and down the cord for the notched wheel, Farina Matthews came into the room. Moving swiftly past the chair, she backhanded him on the bridge of the nose with a fragrant mallet. Tears fell from his eyes and his nose ran and his head filled with some awful decaying smell, but still he did not get up. He covered his face with his hands.

"Don't hit anymore," he said. "It's Charles. Charles the plumber."

She reached for the lamp cord, and the light came on. "You're bleeding."

He breathed into the cave of his hands. "I came back for that shotgun."

"I dreamed of it," she said. "Let's get you out in the kitchen and off these rugs."

Farina Matthews wrapped ice cubes in a rag from beneath the sink, and Charles sat in a chair in the middle of the kitchen floor, like someone getting a haircut. He dropped his head back and pressed the numbing cloth to his nose.

"Is it broken?" she said.

"It was broken a long time ago."

"I gave you a clout, didn't I?"

"Let me see that coat hanger."

She handed it to him, and he held it up to the light. The arms were curved and smooth, and the bottom rail was chamfered in with Phillips-head screws.

"They ain't made the coat that will fall off this," he said, giving it back. "You ever play softball?"

"No."

"You ought to take it up."

"I ought to call the police, if I had any sense . . . I did used to play tennis."

"You got the swing for it."

"Listen, I remembered something about that gun," she said. "You know how you said you didn't have any right to it? Well, it turns out you do, in a way. I hate to say it, but I've always told the truth."

He lowered the ice. "How do you figure?"

"My husband lent your stepfather sixty dollars while holding the gun as surety. That's how we got it. So pay me the money and take the gun and we'll say we're even. I never want to see you again, but I'm sure I will."

"I always thought he just gave it to him."

"That's not how it happened."

"Well, you know better than me." He stood up and got out his billfold, and gave her ten extra for the slit screen. She opened the freezer and stuffed the bills into a coffee can.

"Come," she said, and they went back into the living room, where she took down the gun Charles had brought to her house. Then she turned and saw the other gun lying on the davenport. "Wait a minute."

"I can explain this," said Charles, and he did.

"Did you think I wouldn't know the difference?" She held the shotgun and looked from one gun to the other. "Actually, I might not have."

"I tried for a match. The one I brought is a larger gauge and it has the checkering on the stock. My stepfather's is older, and you can see that in the way the wood's gone sort of honey-colored. And his has the thumb safety, behind the barrels."

"Which is which?"

"The one you've always had is on the davenport. The other one you can keep, if you want something over the fireplace."

"That's not necessary."

"Well, no, but I'm just saying. I've got extras."

Charles left the house through the door, with a shotgun in each hand. The stars were bright, with an airplane crossing beneath. He imagined what the people in the plane were doing. A woman was running away, a man was blowing his nose, a child was reading a book upside down. Meanwhile, the pilot tried to remember a song he used to know. Whatever people did down here, they were doing up there. And then they were gone. Unlike Joan, Charles could see no patterns in the stars: no heroes, no animals. Only a random pelting of space.

"I'm here," he said. "Where are you?"

And by *you* he did not mean Joan, and he did not mean Lyris. He didn't know who or what he meant.

He'd always realized too late the ones he wanted and what it would take to keep them.

Farina Matthews sat up long after Charles had gone. The dream that set the record straight about the gun had brought back memories of her dead husband. She sat in the chair where Charles had sat, holding a poem in a frame. It was called "Everything Comes" and had been written by Thomas Hardy about the house in England, Max Gate, that had given her house its name:

> The house is bleak and cold
> Built so new for me!
> All the winds upon the wold
> Search it through for me;
> No screening trees abound,
> And the curious eyes around
> Keep on view for me.

Driving up to a roadhouse called the Clay Pipe Inn, Charles saw Jerry's car. He pulled in, but the tavern door was locked.

"We're closed," said someone behind the door. "Everybody went home."

"You got my brother in there."

"Charles?"

"Yeah, it's me."

"Oh, Christ, hold on."

The bolt shook free and the door opened. Jerry was sitting at the bar rattling dice in a cup. He turned to look when his brother came in. "What happened to you?" he said.

Charles told him all about it. He offered to go get their step-father's gun from the pickup to show Jerry, but the bartender said guns were not allowed in the tavern, which seemed reasonable, in the abstract.

The phone rang in its cubbyhole beneath the liquor bottles, and the bartender answered. "We're closed," he said again.

Jerry held up his hands to indicate that he was not taking calls. Kenny, the bartender, smiled. "Yeah . . . he's here." He set the phone on the bar facing Jerry and ducked under the cord.

"Hello?" said Jerry. "What's up?" He put down the cup of dice and picked up a felt-tip pen. Cradling the phone with his shoulder, he wrote *Octavia P* in bleeding blue letters on a paper napkin. "Listen, honey, I understand that and I'm sorry, but you shouldn't be calling me. The bar has locked its doors. By rights I shouldn't even be here . . . No, that's true. Have you tried that thing I told you about? Just put your foot flat to the floor . . . Well, how do you know if you haven't tried it? . . . No . . . I'm saying no . . ." Staring into space, Jerry covered the mouthpiece with his hand. "Would you guys move off or something? Give me some privacy."

Charles took up the pen and drew a donkey on the napkin, and then he and the bartender went to play pinball. Jerry leaned close to the wooden rail of the bar and spoke into the phone while shielding his mouth from their eyes. A hand-printed sign on the wall above the pinball machine said:

> If merely "feeling good" could decide, drunkenness would
> be the supremely valid human experience.
>
> — William James, Psychologist

"You know what he's doing?" said the bartender. He drew back on the plunger of the game, the theme of which was the adventures of Oliver North. Painted on the glass façade, Fawn Hall slipped documents into her boots.

Charles shook his head.

"Talking her to sleep."

"No lie."

"I wish it was. I've seen it before. It's the saddest thing imaginable."

"What's he supposed to be, her boyfriend?"

"She calls him and he tells stories into the phone, and beyond that I ask no questions."

"Jesus Christ."

"It ain't natural, whatever it is."

Jerry hung up the phone and sat for a moment before coming over, waving the paper napkin. "What's this you drew — a dog?"

"It's a jackass," said Charles.

"I don't see that." He showed the drawing to the bartender. "What do you think, Kenny?"

"A zebra would have been my guess."

"You're blind," said Charles.

"Well, what are these marks supposed to be?"

"Obviously you know nothing about commercial art."

"Maybe not, but I know a zebra from a jackass."

"And what does that make Jerry?"

"Oh, well, *he's* a jackass. But this, I would have to say, is a zebra."

"We're friends," said Jerry. "You guys don't even know what grade she's in."

"You, Gerald, are walking on an earthquake."

"Remains to be seen."

Charles looked at the pinball machine. Oliver North glared, gap-toothed, patriotic to a fault. "What does she want with a friend like you?"

"I don't understand all of it," said Jerry. "People think she's so together, but she's what you might call a bundle of insecurities."

"I'm taking my guns and going."

The remark reminded them all that it was time to go home.

In the parking lot, Charles showed the old shotgun to Jerry, who picked it up and sighted idly along the ridge between the barrels.

"Really this should go to Bebe. He was her dad."

"I feel like he was mine too," said Charles.

"Yes, because he lasted the longest. We must have been born under bad stars."

"I'll tell you who was born under the bad star, and that's Colette."

"Yes," said Jerry. "I think you're right."

Charles went home. He could not resist opening and closing the barn doors to admire the work that he and Lyris and Micah had done. They had made themselves a team; it hadn't gone too badly. Hearing the doors, the goat came down from the back porch and paced in the long grass. She snorted softly, favoring one of her legs.

"I just may have bought myself a lame goat," said Charles out loud.

Still no Lyris. Her bed was empty under a quilt of green and blue. He called the sheriff's office and left a message and then sat at the kitchen table cleaning the shotgun. He unclipped the barrels from the stock and worked a patch of flannel through each one with a dowel rod. It was five minutes to two. He oiled the flannel and ran it through again. Then he took the cloth and cleaned the breechblock, the triggers, the guard, and the stock. The phone rang. It was Earl the deputy, reporting that Lyris hadn't been in any accidents. Charles thanked him and hung up. The two parts of the gun lay on the table. He wondered if she had run away, but then thought not, given the good day they'd had together. So he figured she must have gone for a ride, and if her absence worried him — as it did — it was a small sample of the worry he had given to others when he was young and even when he was older. Or, while he was on the subject, the worry he must've caused Farina Matthews tonight before she smacked him with the hanger. He thought that Montaigne had got it right: what he did not admire in himself he was in no position to get rid of. It was ahead of him, always, guiding his moves. He made a cup of tea, cut another square of flannel with a pair of rusted scissors, and cleaned the gun again.

7 · Micah

EVOLUTION HAD MADE a lot of trouble at school.
There had been night meetings at which fundamentalists
from another state argued that it should not be taught. In
the meantime, Micah's teacher had to take down the poster of
prehistoric men. The children were not privy to the meetings,
but they noted a new sense of purpose in the teachers. The
endless days for once seemed to hold an importance to the
outside world. Micah's parents had their own opinions. Descended from single-celled organisms or not, Charles said,
everyone had to pay the electric bill or lose the house. Since
Republicans were against evolution, however, he felt honor
bound to be for it. Joan attended one of the meetings, in a long
dress and airy perfume, and afterward she said that far from
disproving the presence of God, the old changes showed
the elegance of his work. Eventually evolution won, and the
teacher taped the poster up again, and the children cheered the
return of the naked extinct men striding forth, leading with
their chins, as they might cheer the football team at home-
coming.

Maybe this explains what Micah saw when he woke in
Colette's house. The figures from the poster had come to life

and were walking through her living room. Java, Heidelberg, Peking, Broken Hill, Solo, Swanscombe. They sang and carried firesticks and flint scrapers. They lumbered thoughtfully, as if they had miles to go. Of course, they would not think in terms of miles. Solo Man banged into a standing brass ashtray, and Micah jumped from the davenport, too late to catch it. Swanscombe Man looked at the fallen ashtray, stepped over it, and followed the others out the door. Then Micah's grandmother came into the room, taking her turn in line as if she were the latest model of human development. She turned on the overhead light, which shone soft yellow through a bowl of cut glass.

"Listen," he said. "Do you hear singing?"

She stood the ashtray upright. "That's 'Absterge Domine' on my new sound system."

"Where's Dad?"

"He had to go do something for someone."

Micah looked around the room, wondering whether to tell her what he had seen. He decided to go ahead, since his grandmother was at ease with unusual notions. She believed, for example, that people should eat dirt once in a while to maintain their health.

She sat down. "They're ghosts," she said. "You don't have to worry about them. What they want, they don't want from you. Once in the hallway I seen an old farmer with a box of matches. Another time there was an Indian wearing snowshoes and a red hat with a string on it. Ghosts can't help where they go. This house just gets them. I think at one time it was an important place."

"I can't sleep."

She went out to the kitchen and brought back a tray bearing a bottle, a pitcher, two glasses, and some rocks. She gave him one of the rocks to look at.

Micah guessed it was an arrowhead, but his grandmother

said more like a knife. She held it in her long, wrinkled fingers. "See all these little hone marks along the blade? That's how you know it was worked by human hand."

"Where'd you find it?"

"When they dug the sewer line, why, these were just laying on the ground. People walk by this sort of thing every day, but they're not looking."

"What did they cut with it?"

"Skins, I imagine. Deer and buffalo and so forth. Everybody's got to eat."

"Not ghosts."

"That's true. But even they want to eat. They're always hungry and they don't know why. And it's too bad."

She poured brandy and water into the glasses. "Go to sleep."

"I'm not tired."

"Drink this and you will be."

"It tastes like blackberries."

"That's right."

"Tell me about ghosts."

They drank from their respective glasses while Colette told of traveling ghosts, who howl along with train whistles — Micah must have heard some of them, living as he did by the tracks — and paper ghosts, who mess up documents, and jealous ghosts, who call on the telephone and ask for people who aren't there. Also touching ghosts, who give the shivers, and bridge ghosts, such as the so-called Baby Mahoney, and vain ghosts, which are the only ones that can be seen, and mumbling ghosts, who are responsible for the phenomenon of one person turning to another in a quiet room and asking, "Did you say something?"

"Do the men you married ever come back as ghosts?" said Micah.

"No."

"They say Morris hit a train."

"Eugene hit the train, who would have been your grandfather. Morris just fell over one day. He was before Eugene. The last to go was Jack Sandover."

"I'm scared."

She nodded, seemed far away. "Fear is a hard thing."

"I don't know what to do about it."

"Finish your drink and say goodnight."

She picked up the tray and left. Micah was alone in the living room. The music had stopped, but at least she had left the light on. He stretched out on the davenport. Wakefulness was like a fire inside him, and if he did nothing but lie still, he knew very well, it would soon be burning out of control. Adults seemed not to understand how desperate a child could get being awake when no one else was.

Maybe he should get a book. A cupboard by the kitchen door held a hardback guide to game animals. He took it down and returned to the davenport, where he lay on his back with his right ankle balanced on his left knee. He rested the book on his stomach and flipped the pages. The photographs were black-and-white and nothing special. The porcupine looked like a wig tossed in the grass, and the jaguar's eyes were glassy from the light of a flashbulb. Micah was surprised to see the porcupine listed as a game animal. Most of the pages had no pictures, and many contained maps of North America with boring shaded areas. Impatiently he turned pages, arriving at last at the inside of the back cover. The paper had split, revealing a coarsely webbed backing. So this was how books were made.

Micah closed the cover, behind which lay an empty triangle framed on either side by his legs and across the top by his right calf. He opened the cover again and the space was hidden. His legs, in other words, formed the archway of a mountain pass, and the book cover was a crude wooden door that had been fitted into the stone by robbers. The three robbers had dismantled a cabin and set the door into rock, and now they were coming home. He spoke their conversation softly to himself.

"I'm so tired I could collapse right into bed."

"Unfortunately, we have no beds."

"It doesn't matter, since I can't sleep anyway."

"You can't sleep because you don't try to sleep."

"Maybe I will sleep on the stove."

"We must steal some beds."

"You will burn yourself sleeping on the stove."

"That would be true if we had firewood, but as you remember, we're fresh out."

"We must remind ourselves to steal beds to sleep in and wood to burn in the stove."

He muttered on, but the game would have been more entertaining if he had had small figures to move about. He thought he remembered seeing some of his father's or Jerry's or Bebe's old cowboys in a coffee can on the porch. The cowboys were made of yellow rubber, and their feet were joined by flat platforms in the shape of a peanut. In his mind's eye, the can was in a cardboard box, along with a piston of an old car that was no longer around. But he knew he might find no piston and no coffee can and no cardboard box. Maybe there were ghosts who made you believe that the things you wanted were in one place while they were moving them to another.

One of the most oppressive times for Micah was when Joan or Charles ordered him to help find something. Sometimes by moaning and kicking and looking where they had already looked he could get himself dismissed from the assignment. Until then, it was like purgatory, or a prison sentence of no fixed term. He would picture them all growing older — Joan stooped and fragile, Charles with a long gray beard, himself a tall and handsome young man — while doomed to the eternal hunt for the savings deposit book or the corkscrew or the little key that would fit onto the inset stems of the radiators if only someone could find it. And what about Lyris? What would she be in the years to come? A scientist, an aviator — something beyond their expectations.

He sighed and got up and went out to the porch through the door that the prehistoric singers had used. He closed the door silently and nudged the light switch, but the bulb had burned out. This would not matter if the yellow cowboys were where he thought they were. The street light filtering through the large slack porch screens would be enough. The box should be behind a defunct water heater that had been cut open for the storage of magazines. He found the box, found the piston with its lank shaft like a broken wing, found the coffee can full of . . . marbles. He clawed through them, making a glassy racket, as if the cowboys might be beneath them. Moving sadly back to the door, he opened a wooden cabinet to confirm that his chrome six-shooter was still there. Yes — at least something could be counted on. He picked up the shining gun and took hold of the doorknob, only to find that the door had locked when he had come out.

Micah thought of calling for his grandmother. Instead, he spoke her name in a low and confident voice that she might not have heard if she were standing beside him. "Grandma," he said calmly and generously, as if bringing to her attention in the kindest way some obvious flaw in her logic. "Grand-mother." And what difference did it make? The night he was afraid of was inside the house, not outside. The darkness of the country could be fearsome, with its rumors of bridge ghosts and of wild cats that would maim the unsuspecting pet. Here in town, darkness was just a name that could not hide the relative wealth of light. Micah went down the swaybacked planks of the steps. These town people didn't know how good they had it. There were streetlamps and house lights and a yellow traffic beacon that flashed and swayed on a cable over the street. The town was a playground of electricity, and he had the whole place almost to himself. A car rolled past so slowly that it seemed he might reach out and stop its tires with his hand. On the car radio, a woman sang in a deep and weary voice, "I think I lost it, let me know if you come across it . . ." Micah wondered how he must look to the driver — small but dangerous, a figure of mystery, a kid in the night with a pistol in his hand. He knew that adults sometimes mistook toy guns for real ones. In the city, police might even shoot you for having a cap pistol. Of course, the driver might not have seen him. He could not rule that out.

When the car had gone he crossed the street, which seemed to put years between him and Colette. Standing on the sidewalk, he thought of her as someone he had seen long ago, and he realized with a faint tremor that he should be standing beside the house calling her name or lobbing pebbles against her window. It occurred to him that he had split into two personalities, one of whom was trying to get back into the house while the other could do whatever it wanted.

A man sat in his living room, watching television and drinking from a mug. Micah stuck the gun into the waist of his jeans, cupped his hands around his eyes, and leaned against the window. On the television screen, a man and a woman with no clothes moved about, their bodies so large they might have been circus folk. They stalked each other around a wide bed. Micah had wondered about sex. Maybe they were about to launch into it.

He took one hand from the window, intending to scratch his back with his thumb, and his forehead clunked against the glass. The man got up and stood with his back to the television. Micah hurried from the window to hide behind a bank of split wood beside the house. A spider walked on his wrist, and he shook it off. The front door opened. The man looked dumpy and confused, nothing like the characters sporting on the television. He wore a sweatshirt from an automotive store.

An orange cat ran out of the house, and the man called, "Who's out there? Terry?" He drank from the mug and looked up and down the street. "If it's Terry, you better show yourself. I mean it, honey."

Micah waited until the man was in the house before walking carefully away. He passed the building that used to be the barbershop and another building that used to be the grocery store and was now said to be teeming with mice. He wondered what time it was. It might be midnight or it might be three-thirty or it might be fifty-hundred. The drying fan of the grain elevator ran all night this time of year. He listened to its thriving, empty sound. A ladder ran to the top of the silo, and he made a mental note that he would climb it someday to survey the town and the fields around it. He might yell his name — *Micah! I am Micah!* — though no one likes a showoff. For now, he walked to the top of the ramp that led into the covered alleyway and sat down on the concrete, his back to the big wooden doors. Kernels of corn littered the ramp. Scooped into a basket, they would make a fair amount. A person could earn extra money just picking up the grain that others had spilled in this town. It was surprising how many adult thoughts you could generate when no adults were around to remind you that you were not them. He would give his money to the bank, in front of which a cottontail rabbit now hopped uncertainly along the sidewalk. Micah took out his gun and trained it on the rabbit but made no shooting sound. Like his father, he would never eat rabbit.

It was high time to go back, but then he never should have left in the first place, so he kept walking. In a barn he saw an old Camaro, bleached of color, with empty sockets where its headlights should have been. On a curving street he saw a low building with a tall chimney. Charles always said that the bricklayers who made the chimney must have been working by the hour.

A pickup came down off the highway with light beaming from the roof lamps, followed by a car and a ton truck. Going where, he could not guess. Nothing was open now. As a matter of fact, very little was open in the daytime. He walked back to the elevator as the three vehicles gathered in the gravel lot where the restaurant used to be. Micah and Charles had come into town one day to watch the restaurant get knocked down and trucked away in pieces. Later they had gone to another town for dinner.

A man got out of the car and checked his watch. Micah went over and struck up a conversation.

"Town's quiet tonight, wouldn't you say?"

The man looked at him. He wore overalls and a whistle on a string around his neck. "Get out of here," he said.

Another man jumped down from the bed of the ton truck. He had a sheet of notebook paper with squares and arrows penciled in. "The way I figure it, Vincent, we space ourselves out on the perimeter and walk inward."

"What happens when we see one?" said Vincent, the man with the whistle.

"We shoot."

"At each other. That's your plan." He took the page and looked it over and folded it and tore it up. "That's Leo's plan."

"What are you hunting?" said Micah.

"Who asked you?"

"I'll go along."

"No you won't."

"Who brought the kid?" said the driver of the pickup. "Whose kid are you? Are you Kevin's?"

"I wonder where Kevin is," said Leo, whose plan lay torn to pieces on the gravel.

"Kevin's got the dog. It's pointless without him."

Micah told them his parents' names and where they lived and his grandmother's name and where she lived.

"Get home."

"I have a book of game animals back at the house."

"Go curl up with it."

The man in the pickup said, "You have no idea how to speak to a child. Son. Listen to old Bob. Go home."

"I have good eyes."

"We're proud of you," said Vincent. He took Micah by the back of his shirt and pushed him down the sidewalk. The chrome six-shooter fell on the ground.

"That's my gun," said Micah.

"Well, pick it up."

Micah retrieved the pistol. "At least you could tell me what you're hunting."

"If I tell you, will you go home?"

"Maybe."

"Fox."

Micah went back to Colette's house, and the three men waited for Kevin with their engines running. One of them turned on the radio, picking up the big station out of Little Rock. Once the men had left for a weekend in Las Vegas at the same time another plane was leaving for Arkansas, but that's as close as any of them had ever got to Little Rock. Leo had had a plan for Vegas, just as he had a plan for hunting foxes. He thought he knew most of what there was to know about baccarat, and therefore he lost a thousand dollars, just like that. There was nothing wrong with his plan in that case, it was just that he was unlucky at cards. He was unlucky at everything, he said so himself, and why he had gone to Las Vegas was a question no one could answer.

8 · Joan

JOAN SAT in a red leather chair in the lobby of the Astrid Hotel, listening to a woman playing a harp. She rested her arms on the sides of the chair, palms up, as if waiting for coins to fall from the gilded ceiling. She didn't think her speech in the ballroom had gone all that well, but it was over. The music made her feel better. Her face cooled in the hotel evening.

Sound did not travel easily in the ballroom. All she had heard was the echo of her words; all she had seen was darkness. Sweat collected under her eyes, trickled down her neck. It was probably lucky that she had no makeup to put on beforehand. Someone had replaced her compact with a nutcracker and a dozen walnuts. Charles or Micah, she figured. Lyris had not been in the family long enough to learn about the hours of contentment to be had from playing tricks on Joan.

She had gone on with her speech, the theme being that centuries of breeding had not robbed domestic animals of their taste for freedom. She showed slides and cited the experiments of Ward and Wolper at the University of Illinois. She gave examples — perhaps too many examples. The conclusion was a reading from Rudyard Kipling: "Then he goes out to the Wet Wild Woods or up the Wet Wild Trees or on the Wet Wild Roofs, waving his wild tail and walking by his wild lone." Afterward, two people asked where she had done her graduate work, and she explained that all her knowledge came from years of lay observation.

She rose from the red chair and drifted down a hallway to the pay phones. No one answered at home, but the distance between Joan and her family seemed to guard them. Things could only be all right. There was a lounge next to the telephones, and she went in and ordered a Moscow Mule.

"You're just in time," said the bartender. "The hypnotist is about to start his act."

Joan drank the Mule and looked around. The black tables were taken by convention-goers, listing slightly, with glazed eyes, as if they had already been hypnotized.

"Good crowd," she said.

The bartender shrugged. "I haven't counted."

"What are they after?"

"Who knows? This is my third week at the Astrid. A hotel bar is different."

"It's because the people are only passing through."

"Well, I think that's right. They're away from home for a night or two. They laugh and talk, and the ones who get hypnotized wonder what they did while they were under. People argue, they throw up their hands, they stalk out. You wouldn't believe how many. They don't know each other very well to begin with. The arguments tend to begin right back there in the corner. Then they spread."

"I think they want to be changed."

"Who?"

"Everybody."

"Yeah?"

"Don't you?"

"Hmm," he said. He slid wet glasses into the compartments of a blue plastic crate. "You're asking what I want or what I think they want?"

"What you want."

"Now that's a question. I'd have to consider it."

"That's what I want."

A waitress came up with a pencil behind her ear. "Candy, what do people want?" said the bartender.

"A little loving, I suppose," she said.

The bartender poured liquor through a red spout with sharp downward thrusts of the bottle, and the waitress took the drinks out among the tables.

"Changed into what, though?" asked the bartender.

"I guess I'll know it when it happens," said Joan. "But now I'm beginning to wonder if it *will* happen. To be made something good. And I'm not young. I've been waiting a long time already. And whenever I think I've found it, I realize later that I was wrong. Do you know that the universe is expanding?"

"Well, I've heard that."

"They believe that the end of the universe, which is so far away in the first place, is getting farther away all the time. And not slowly but quickly. I mean, it's *moving*. While here we sit with our small concerns. Funny, isn't it? Sometimes I feel like whatever I'm supposed to be is tacked to the back wall of the universe and moving away from me at the speed of light."

"You shouldn't come in here alone," said the bartender. "In a way it goes against my interests to say so, but if you want my advice, don't. Otherwise you end up having thoughts like you're having."

"Why, because I'm a woman?"

"Men are worse."

"I think this way all the time."

"There's a pool on the twelfth floor."

"Maybe I'll head up there."

"Also a health club. You could ride the stationary bike if you don't like swimming."

The hypnotist performed on a small tiled dance floor near the jukebox. He walked back and forth before the tables, choosing volunteers. A silver lighter provided the flame by which he mesmerized them. He lifted the lighter and told his subjects to imagine that it was the moon rising. "How do you feel?" he said.

"Sleepy."

"Under the influence."

"Angry."

"Hypnotized."

The hypnotist asked the angry man what the problem was and, after much back-and-forth, got him to explain his suspicion that his ex-wife was sending blank postcards to his house. Not one or two, but many. The hypnotist tried to convince the man that his ex-wife was in the audience and willing to listen, but this illusion failed to take hold. Then he directed the man to make his body completely rigid so that he could be laid like a plank across two chairs. This worked, and the audience applauded politely but seemed disappointed not to be able to hear the man have it out with the phantom of his ex-wife. Joan left the bar feeling more hypnotized than the man whose fate it was to be bombarded with blank postcards.

She walked through the lobby. It seemed that hours had passed since she had relaxed in the chair by the harp. The concierge waved her over to his desk and said that a doctor had been looking for her. He gave her a vial of pills that the doctor had left and bid her goodnight. She went up to her room and put on her swimsuit and a robe. Maybe the doctor had come to the city on business of his own, attending another conference in another hotel. Maybe he had a patient who had taken sick in the city. There were a hundred reasons for him to be here, no doubt. She rode up to the health club in the elevator.

The swimming pool was deserted except for a young woman reading a chemistry book, who handed Joan a towel. It was a beautiful place at night. Yellow light played on the water, and willowy plants pressed against windows looking out on the tall darkened buildings of the city. The chlorine smelled strong enough to make the pool seem clean but not so strong as to be unpleasant. Joan went down a ladder into the warm water, which dissolved the events of the night. The echo of her words, the drops of her sweat, the hypnotist, the postcards — nothing could penetrate the plane of the water or follow the stroke of her swimming. She lay on her back, kicking her legs intermittently as her hands gently turned, pulling her forward. Her submerged ears heard a sound like breathing. Whether it was the sound of the hotel or of the city or of the universe flying apart she could not say. A mosaic of blue mirrors covered the vaulted ceiling, so that she could watch the broken progress of her body far below. She saw her swimming self as if through the unbiased eyes of a bird. At the deep end, she folded into the water and kicked toward the white lights near the bottom.

The day of the tornado, Joan and Micah were returning from the grocery store in Charles's van. Like the van he had now, it was full of tools and pipes and metal boxes. The tornado appeared on the other side of town, and seeing it, Joan drove into the driveway of an abandoned farm. Carrying Micah, she ran to the house. The front door swung open. It had been kicked in earlier by Dr. Palomino, whom they found sitting in a wing chair in the living room, watching the funnel cloud through the windows. The tail yawed, churning up dirt and lumber, and every now and then a fierce light flashed within the flexing cloud. If they spoke — and they must have spoken — they perhaps noted how chance would dictate that the tornado would not come their way. There were so many other ways it might go. The funnel swelled as it moved across a bean field, ripping up plants and clods and spinning them out as silver powder. Joan and the doctor could not find any basement stairs, and so they lay down in a central hallway with Micah between them. A gateleg table supported by an intricate platform of spindles could be seen in the next room. Joan got up and tried to shove the table aside so it would not come crashing into them. The legs caught on the floorboards, and Joan seized the table between the drop leaves and flipped it over. When she returned to the hallway, Micah said, "The ratlike creature slithers to and fro." The strangeness of the remark did not sink in until later. The wind became very loud, and the house scraped off its foundation. Glass fell from the windows. When the timbers settled, Joan picked up Micah and carried him out to the van, followed by the doctor. The doctor started the engine and cranked the wheel, but the tornado came down the trough of a grove and shoveled the van toward the barn with such force that his steering became meaningless. Joan sat with her arms wrapped around Micah, and the doctor abandoned the driver's seat, stationing himself between the boy and the dashboard, shielding him from whatever lay ahead. The van skidded along, nose in the ground. Lost in the whirlwind, they could see nothing. The corner of the barn materialized only when they hit it. The van twisted like an awl held in the grip of an unsteady carpenter. Tools and groceries flew against the metal walls. It occurred to Joan, as it must have to the doctor, that a van full of plumbing equipment might rank among the worst places to be during a tornado. Then the wall of the barn gave way, and the van moved through its broken boards and through another wall and into the round and slatted space of an empty wooden silo. The doctor said that if the silo went they would be completely fucked, and they got out of the van and left the silo through its door. The sky was pale blue and blurred by a rain of dirt and water. A rainbow wrapped around the grove. Joan held Micah and whispered in his ear, reciting God's promise in Genesis 9: "And it shall come to pass, when I bring a cloud over the earth, that the bow shall be seen in the cloud: And I will remember my covenant, which is between me and you and every living creature . . . and the waters shall no more become a flood to destroy all flesh."

The doctor stood at the pool's edge, offering a towel, and Joan climbed the steps and dried her hair. With the towel covering her eyes, she shed the tears that she might have cried during the tornado if she had not been so busy trying to keep Micah alive. But this did not really get at why she was crying. It had something to do with the rainbow they had seen afterward. Maybe she no longer believed in covenants, that one or any other. What if the rules and verses she had lived by, or tried to, didn't mean what she thought they did?

Joan pressed the towel against the tears she did not want the doctor to see. Then she continued to massage her hair for a long time.

She dried her arms and legs. "What are you doing here?" she said.

"I consult with a doctor in the city from time to time," he said. "And there is a patient, not my patient, but she wanted me to look at the charts. So, since I was going to be here anyway —"

"I don't believe it," she said. She handed him the towel and he folded it. That he was fully clothed and she wore only a swimsuit might have put her at a disadvantage, but she didn't feel that way at all, for the one in street clothes is always odd man out at poolside.

"It's true, though," said the doctor. "An intriguing case in which the patient is having difficulty swallowing food. There is an esophageal stricture which is fairly common — you may know it as Schatzki's ring — but this would seem not to be Schatzki's, because of certain other symptoms that we need not delve into."

"You came to see me," said Joan.

"The pool is closing," said the young woman with the text-book.

The doctor and Joan went down to Joan's room in the elevator. Wearing the hotel robe, she took little bottles of vodka and tonic from a refrigerator in the bathroom, and she made drinks, and they sat by the windows in the dark.

"Joan, I've got a love in me that isn't going anywhere," the doctor said, holding his vodka in both hands, with his elbows set on his knees. "Ever since the tornado, I've just been idling, like an automobile engine. And all because of you. I've even taken to looking at pornographic films."

"I had no idea," she said.

"It's not me," he said. "It just isn't me at all."

"No, I had some idea," she admitted.

"When I saw you swimming, I said to myself, 'If I had three lifetimes, I would give two of them up for her.'"

Joan cracked walnuts, pushing the shells carefully aside with the edge of her hand. "But you only have one."

"And this is where it is," said the doctor.

"Can you make me better?"

"You're gold inside. Don't you know that?"

She thought of the hypnotized man's story of his broken marriage and how the worst part must have been the blankness of the postcards. If the woman who'd left him had written something, no matter how bleak, then at least he would have some measure of what he had done. But the emptiness would bother anyone. What did she want? What had she become? Why so *many* cards? Considering these questions, Joan felt her own identity evaporating. She analyzed her actions as she would those of someone she did not know. If she were going to send the doctor away, she would not have invited him in. If she were going to send him away, she would not have dried herself with a towel from his hands.

"No one ever said I was gold inside," said Joan.

A moth landed on the glass while they sat eating walnuts and drinking. The room was on the seventh floor, high for a moth to fly. It was not drawn to the light, because the light was off. It was a large moth with feathery antennae. The papery brown wings closed and opened in the slow rhythm of respiration. It would be too much to say that they would not have gone ahead without this reminder of indifferent nature. People looking for a sign will find one soon. But once the moth had landed, they began to kiss, and then to undress. Joan untied the white cord of her robe, pulled it slowly from its loops, wrapped it loosely around a fist, dropped the terry coil on the table. She wondered what day it was. They moved to the bed. Their clothes were on the carpet, in city light. She wondered why it should all seem so inevitable, as if they were inside the funnel again, spinning down. His hands touched her skin and she let go of the memory. It was always this way, and always would be.

An hour passed, an hour and ten minutes. The night passed. Joan and the doctor dressed and went down to the lobby. If they felt shame, no one could have known. Joan showed the doctor the harp and strummed its strings, although she could play only the piano. They crossed a red and gray carpet with their heads held high and went out the revolving doors. The doctor offered his arm, and Joan took it. A panel truck came down the street; a bundle of newspapers landed on the sidewalk. When the truck had passed, the doctor raised the fibrous blue band that held the bundle together while Joan knelt to pull a newspaper free. They walked on, looking at dazed mannequins in the windows of a store, and when they reached the end of the block they turned the corner.

❧ Sunday

9 · Lyris

I T WAS AFTER MIDNIGHT. How had it gotten so late? She must have slept. Car lights moved toward them in lonely pairs on a narrow road between ditches. Lyris had no idea where they were or where they were going. Follard was telling her about an old friend who had driven so drunk sometimes that she would see two pairs of headlights for every car; all she could do was steer between them. "Lucky to be alive," he said. Follard had seen too many people ruined by liquor. Lyris admitted she had tried the spiked chocolate. The headlights did not look double to her, but they vibrated.

Follard took her to see a big grain operation out in the country. Boxcars were lined up on the rail siding, and Lyris thought of Charles's talk of grain, making its way to the river. He seemed to want to know more about agriculture than he did — as if it were his duty, being from farm country. Follard circled the towering silos, his tires throwing gravel, until Lyris grew dizzy and closed her eyes. When she opened them, she saw an old watchman crossing the parking lot with a baseball bat over his shoulder.

"Here comes somebody," she said.

"I see him."

Lyris waved at the man slowly, as if her hand were under water.

The watchman returned the wave of the girl in the car as if conceding the harmlessness of her adventure. He returned to the office, where he leaned the bat in a corner next to a refrigerator, from which he took a quart of beer. He uncapped it and drank. One of the cats had walked on his game of solitaire and mixed up the cards; there would be no getting it back.

"That's just great," he said to a cat gnawing its toes on an old leather chair. "Is that right?" he said. "Then who was it?"

The old man squared up the cards and shuffled. His son was a bartender who every once in a while would drop by the elevator on his way home from work. Once he had brought two dancers to see the elevator, and the old man had run corn into the pit from overhead for their amusement. The women were amazed by the force of it and by the tumbling nails that were mixed with the corn because it was salvage grain. Sixteen-penny, the old man had estimated. So polite they were, like college students. They called him sir and said that earlier in the night his son had ejected from the bar a man who was as big as Sinbad the Sailor.

The watchman dealt and played a new hand. Then he walked through the feed room, where the big potbellied grinder was shaking corn kernels to dust. White powder caked the grinder, drifted from the rafters. The watchman crossed the alleyway to a metal shed. Inside was a mound of salt pellets many times taller than himself. He sighed and began shoveling pellets into a large paper sack with a hand scoop. When the sack was two-thirds full, he lifted it onto a portable scale, read the gauge, and added pellets until the pointer floated at sixty pounds. Then he tied the sack closed with string and carried it to another part of the storeroom.

There would be no end to the work. He felt that he could shovel and weigh and tie for the rest of his years, not so many now, and the mountain of salt would not get one pellet smaller. Strange, how it took so much to make so little.

"Sinbad the Sailor," he said.

Follard drove carelessly, turning every so often, with no apparent route in mind. Eventually they arrived at a little bridge on a twisting gravel road. They stepped from the car and stood with their hands in their coat pockets. Lyris recognized neither the road nor the iron frame of the bridge. The river moved along, tight whirlpools forming on its surface. The moon shone above the lacing of cottonwood branches.

"Is it true you burned your parents' house?" The question was too loud.

"Who, me?"

"That's what my father said."

Follard looked out over the river. "The court ruled it was an accident. People forget the evidence. They brought in a fire marshal who testified that a kerosene heater might go off that way if it was not maintained. And believe me when I say ours was not maintained."

"Did they die? Your parents, I mean."

"No. She shot him, but he lived. I can tell you this much: if you want to see a miserable backbiting spectacle, try bringing two fire marshals into court with differing opinions."

"Who shot who?"

Follard gripped the iron bars of the bridge and rocked back as if trying to pull them down.

"My mother. Shot my father. The fire was just a coincidence. I jumped out of the house when I heard the shooting, and there was no fire at that point. Or if there was, it hadn't come up to the second floor. I'm not saying I didn't smell smoke. But I knew that whatever was going on in the house was something to get away from. The county attorney couldn't accept that no one would get jail time out of such a mess. They acquitted my mother on self-defense. They acquitted me because their theory of arson required me to be in two places at once. My father had been shot and burned, so I guess the judge figured probation and a restraining order were enough for him."

Lyris began climbing the ironwork of the bridge. "Where are they now?"

"My mom moved to Michigan and my old man ended up in New Mexico. For a while he wrote letters saying I should come out there because of the sky or something. Then he stopped writing. I was supposed to live with my aunt and uncle, but they were decent enough to set me up in my own place."

A metal plate about two feet wide ran along the top of the bridge. Lyris lay down on it on her back, feeling the round caps of the bolts through her clothes. To her left and nine feet down was the road; to her right and twenty feet down was the river.

"You can't go by what people say," said Follard. "They always believe the worst thing. It's like when you broke out of that barn the other night. A common response would be 'Well, there must be a reason she's in there. Maybe she deserved to be locked up.' But I didn't think that."

"I was wearing my mother's dress," she said.

"Regardless of whose dress," said Follard. He climbed halfway up the bridge and rested his arms near the crown of Lyris's head. She could not see him but could hear his voice close to her ears. He spoke softly. "Be careful Baby Mahoney doesn't reach up and take you by the leg."

"I don't know who that is. I've only lived here since summer."

"I can fill you in," said Follard. "Twenty years ago, on this very night — that's how you tell it — a baby named Mahoney fell into the river. The parents got careless and lost their baby."

Lyris turned over and cupped her face in her hands. "You lie."

"Well, yeah, I lie. 'Cause it's only a story."

"I don't like it."

"Just listen. The baby swam or floated for miles and crawled out of the river into the woods. There might have been an animal that helped him. I don't tell it as well as some do. But he grew up in the wild and never learned anything about human beings. To him our ways are a mystery."

Lyris heard her own voice as if it were coming from across the road or up in a tree. "So why would he grab my leg?"

"He's older now," said Follard. "Remember, this was twenty years ago. But he always comes back to the bridge. He lurks around, with feelings he doesn't understand."

"I have to get home."

"Well, I would take you, but the car's out of gas. Or it's thrown a rod, or the key's in the trunk, or there is no car. This is another story that I'm telling now, and this one is true. He wanted to take her home but could not, and therefore, with nothing better to do . . . You see where I'm going."

Lyris pushed up onto her knees. She swayed, a little drunk, a little afraid, a little mad. "You can't make me stay."

He kept his arms folded on the bridge. He didn't seem concerned or angry. Moonlight reflected in his eyes. "Look around. You don't even know where you are. If you had a map, it would not help you. You have no point of reference."

She climbed down the outside of the bridge and stood on a narrow ledge. It was not a far drop to the river; it might even be a pleasant jump in the summer. Follard descended too, but on the inside of the bridge. They eyed each other through a lattice of iron bars.

"Be careful," he said.

Follard's fingers came through the bridge and caught her wrist. His purpose was uncertain, since the spaces were too small for him to pull her through. His fingernails pressed into her skin, but his eyes stayed tranquil. He slid his free hand through the next higher space and transferred her wrist to it. He repeated the maneuver; she saw her hand rising, as if it were no part of her. Evidently he hoped to pull her up and over the top of the bridge. She bit his knuckles, and he called her a crude name. She jumped from the bridge, pushing back, raising her arms, hitting the water with a glassy crash. The depth of the river was unknown to her, and drifting down, she did not touch the bed. What a world it was underwater, ringed by cold and darkness. When she broke to the surface, treading water, Follard was coming down the ditch from the bridge. The current carried her, and she angled to the bank on the side away from him. Follard lifted fence wire and bent under it. Lyris pulled herself from the water, using the branches of a fallen tree.

"Come back, Lyris," he said. "If you'd just hold still, I would take you home."

The air glowed with moonlight. It shone on the blue sleeves of his coat and on the river between them. He did not enter the water — maybe he was afraid — but turned and hurried back up to the bridge. She climbed the steep and muddy bank. The thin dead branches of the tree scratched her face. Follard crossed the bridge. In a moment he would be on her side of the river.

Lyris ran — away from the road, parallel to the water. Follard called after her. He said this was crazy, she would get lost, don't make him chase her. When she could not hear him any longer, she rested under a tree where its trunk fanned into roots. She untied the laces of her shoes, removed them, and peeled off her socks. Her hands were shaking. She wrapped her bare feet in the lining of her coat, kneading toes and soles. Leaves rustled; the moon laid silver stripes on the ground. An owl glided down a corridor of trees, pulled up short, and settled on a branch. On and on the river ran. Lyris told herself not to be afraid. A mile of walking in any direction would bring her to a road. Charles had explained the grid. The river would bring her to a road. The river might be the longest way, but she would not move in a circle. Anyone lost must not move in circles. She left the wet socks beside the tree. Shivering, she put on her shoes, her coat. She rested her back against the tree before going on.

Soon the owl overtook her, flying low beneath the branches with one of her socks snagged in its talons. Its body hung like a weight from the yoke of its wings.

Lyris came to a wooden cabin on a rise above the river. There were matches in a Band-Aid tin above the fireplace, and kindling in a crate. She built a fire and sat before it. A plaque had been set into the fieldstones: THIS HOUSE IS FOR THE COMMON USE OF THE HUNTERS AND HIKERS OF THESE WOODS. LEAVE IT AS YOU WOULD FIND IT. IN MEMORY OF SPRAGUE HEILEMAN B. 1877 D. 1949 BY SON MELVIN AND DAUGHTER JANICE. She laid more wood on the fire and got up. In a chest of drawers she found coveralls and wool socks to wear. On a table she found a box of crackers. The coveralls bunched around her wrists and ankles. The table had been vandalized. People had carved their names into the planks.

He may find me, she thought. She took a metal shovel from the fireplace and put it near her feet under the table.

When someone did come, it was not Follard but Leo, the fox hunter. Lyris didn't know him. He walked in and closed the door and rested a gun against the wall near the fireplace.

He rearranged the burning wood with his boot and stood rubbing his hands. "Hello," he said. "The key bird is out tonight."

Lyris did not understand. "I'm lost," she said. "I'm trying to get home."

The man came over to the table. "What's your name?"

"Lyris Darling."

He ran his hand over his mouth. "One of that bunch," he said softly.

"What is the key bird?"

"That's a joke," he said. "It says — its call would be — 'Key, key, key-riste it's cold.' You see? The way you'd say 'Christ, it's cold' if your teeth were chattering."

"Oh, very good."

"And chattering they are."

"I fell in the river, but I don't even know what one."

"The North Pin," said the man. "Some call it Sprague's Creek."

"Didn't seem like a creek to me."

"Well, no, it wouldn't, in it. It's misleading. What happened?"

"I was on the bridge," she said. "And this guy held my wrist and he wouldn't take me home. He was pulling on me."

"Who?"

"Follard. I don't know his first name."

"The arsonist?"

"He claims not."

"I would not put great stock in what he claims."

"It was stupid to let him drive me."

"Yes, I think it was." The man took out a wooden game call and blew into it. "What's that sound like to you?"

"I don't know," said Lyris.

"It's supposed to sound like a dying rabbit."

"I've never heard a rabbit die, so I wouldn't know what it sounds like."

"Me either."

"Do you have a car?"

"We have cars and trucks," said the man. "We have a dog that knows the fox dens, and when the foxes come out, we put the big lights on them. Or we would if they did come out. The one nest we found tonight has been empty for days. I guess that's why they call them Sly Reynard."

Lyris and the hunter shoveled ashes onto the fire and moved off together through the woods. He said he knew the way. They hiked through an overgrown cemetery with small black stones and under a tree house for deer hunters. Then they were out in the open, beneath the stars, on a lane of short dry grass. The coveralls were warm and dry. The hunter told her his theory of foxhunting and how it differed from what they were doing. He said that crossfire was a legitimate safety issue but one that could be worked out. Perhaps the men could be staggered in such a way that they would not hit each other, or they could call out their positions. Granted, the fox would hear the voices, but by that time it would be on the run anyhow. In a way, the issue of one hunter shooting another was a moot point, because they were using number-two shot, which did not travel more than sixty yards.

As he spoke, a fox slipped from the trees and stood for a moment with one paw raised before trotting away along the lane, nose down, tail high. There wasn't much to it. The fox jumped onto a stone wall, walked on it for a short distance, then dropped off into a field. Lost in his calculations, the hunter did not see the fox, and Lyris couldn't say a word. Everything the hunter had told her so far had led her to suspect that the fox was an entirely hypothetical creature, the behavior of which men could guess about while achieving their true goal of wandering around the woods carrying equipment. To have actually seen a fox altered her point of view in a way that left her too preoccupied to speak or react. She kept moving forward, wet clothes rolled under her arm, and then the fox was gone among the cornstalks and Leo was saying how in some areas foxes are hunted with airplanes, although he was not sure how that worked.

Soon Lyris and Leo saw lights angling through the trees. The rest of the men — Kevin, Vincent, and old Bob — met them at a bend in the grassy lane. The hunting dog was white with brown legs and sidled against Lyris.

"She's the first thing that dog found all night," said old Bob.

"We should try something different," said Leo.

"No," said Vincent. "Did you get the sandwiches?"

"Not yet."

"Well, Jesus Christ."

"I found this young woman. That kid Follard pushed her in the river."

"I'd just as soon smack him as look at him," said Vincent.

Leo drove Lyris home, talking about the Las Vegas trip, how upset he'd been in the desert. She said goodnight in the driveway. Inside, Charles slept at the kitchen table, his head on his arms.

"I'm home," she said. "I'm home."

He sat up and looked around. "What time is it?"

"Three o'clock."

"Is Micah back from school?"

"It's the middle of the night."

He got up and took a clouded glass from the drainboard. Moths circled the ceiling light. Standing before the refrigerator, he poured water from a pitcher. "Well, where's Micah?"

"Upstairs?"

Charles drank half the water and then stared into the glass.

He nodded. "Micah's at my mother's house. And Joan, we know where Joan is."

"We went driving after the game."

"I'm sitting here by the phone."

"I'm sorry."

"Where all'd you drive — St. Louis?"

"I should have called."

"Did we not have a good day? Was there something lacking in the day itself?"

"No," she said. She drew her hands into the sleeves of the coveralls. "It was a good day."

"I know how you feel," said Charles. "Or if I don't, I wonder how you feel. To be dropped into this house, not against your will exactly, but as the last possible place — I see that, I'm not blind to it. Your long-lost mother — I wonder what you make of her. And I'm far from perfect. Far from it. *Perfect* to me is a word with no meaning. I'm just another man in a van. So it must be tempting for you to say, 'Oh hell, what's the use, if this is the place where I've been left.'"

She did not know what to say. He was right in some ways. And she saw the darkness under his eyes. Had he been in a fight?

"But then I think — because, you see, I've given it some thought — how different is your experience from anyone's? On the surface, yeah, it is different. The bomb business is a mystery to us all. We don't know what you've been any more than we know what you will be. But I'm not sure it's so different underneath. Because it's *all* by accident. It's all 'This happens, that happens, and here we are.' I'll be honest with you, even the things I do sometimes don't make sense to me. And the best we can make of it is to remember each other and for God's sake get on the telephone when we're going to be late."

It was not the content of his remarks, which she did not precisely understand, but the length of them that moved her. He had never said so many words to her at once. She moved across the kitchen and fell into his arms. "She didn't want me," she said. "She may not want me still."

"That isn't true, Lyris," said Charles. "You can't go thinking that way. It was not that she didn't want you but that she didn't know you."

He stood rubbing her back in the manner of someone trying to set a flywheel right. If he noticed that she was wearing clothes different from the ones she had left in, he chose not to mention it.

10 · Joan

JOAN AND THE DOCTOR wandered through the morning city arm in arm, like an old couple looking for a store
that might or might not be open anymore. The sunlight
glittered on cars and windows. One storefront offered so
many cameras it made taking pictures seem hopelessly complicated. It had rained during the night, the air offered unusual
depth of field, and down the street they could see the restless
water of a big lake.

The events in the hotel room had been a fleeting dream
brought on by a lost moth, but walking toward the lake in the
light seemed altogether real.

People moved about in shops. A tall man in a canvas apron
cranked out the awnings over a bakery, which failed to wake
the figure lying on the sidewalk in a dirty sleeping bag. A
woman who was smoking carried a bass violin up the steps of
a church. *It is all here,* thought Joan, *the beautiful and the unfortunate.*

The violinist rested her instrument on the top step and took
a last drag before turning a heavy iron ring that opened the
oak-slat door. In front of St. Regina's Hospital, a woman

handed the ribbon of a metallic balloon to a child, and the child let the ribbon go. The breeze carried the balloon up and across the façade of a tall building.

"Now what do we do?" said the woman. "We have no present."

A block down the street, a young man in dark blue sweat clothes with white stripes stood staring thoughtfully into a wire basket of trash. The balloon was a shiny dime in the sky.

They walked on. Dr. Palomino took a raglan hat from his coat pocket and unfolded it and put it on his head. "Cold this morning."

"Oh, doctor."

"What?"

"I feel funny."

He looked around, nodding as if the street had been built according to his specifications. "I could live in this city. Sign on with a hospital, find a townhouse, walk to a store, buy a candy bar and a magazine. I could see it. There's always a demand for competent doctors."

"Your luck," said Joan.

She was wondering whom she loved. Micah. Lyris — she would love her. Children are sponges of love; they can't help taking up every drop. But to love only children is to withdraw from the adult world in a way that does not feel so good. What she felt for Charles was a hard question. When Lyris came, he started doubting everything Joan said and did. He had suspicions he had not had before. Resentment had crept into their lives. He hated to be misled more than anyone she knew. Everyone was out to fool him, everyone but Joan; he had not thought her capable. When they turned away from each other in bed now, it seemed to be a statement. The chores they had once taken on lightheartedly had become ammunition to be used against each other. *Oh Charles*, she thought, *what happened to the fun couple we used to be?* Sometimes life seemed so small she wanted to put it in a ring box and throw it in the tall grass.

"Do my children need me?" the doctor was saying. "I think they need my car. Me, I'm not so sure."

"I've been aching for something like last night," said Joan. "Now that I have it, I'm still aching."

They drank coffee in a restaurant with photographs bearing the splashy signatures of local celebrities. Dr. Palomino theorized about how hard it would be to wait tables. He said that removing the vermiform appendix was easier than taking a plate of soup to a table, because at least the customer in the appendectomy was out cold. Joan said she still had her appendix, and the doctor admitted that many people keep them for life. The main thing to remember when removing them was to count the sponges. Two men sitting in the adjacent booth moved to another booth. Then Dr. Palomino asked if Joan would like to meet the doctor he had mentioned last night.

"I thought you made her up."

"Why would I lie?"

"To avoid saying you came here on my account."

"That is a good reason. And I did lie. There is no patient with Schatzki's ring. But there is a doctor. Her name is Mona Lomasney."

Dr. Palomino called Dr. Lomasney from a pay phone, and away they went, to a neighborhood some distance from downtown. The cab driver smoked a yellow pipe that smelled like burning grapes as he squinted into the sun over a divided highway.

Mona Lomasney had spent her professional life in this city, Dr. Palomino told Joan. St. Regina's had hired her out of college in Montana, and Women and Infants had stolen her from St. Regina's. It was at Women and Infants that she became a star, the second woman ever to win the rarely given Golden

Pyramid. But when morphine went missing, the hospital had no choice but to confront Mona and the other doctors implicated. They had been providing the drug on the side to patients who, because of a new policy, had been switched to nonnarcotic analgesics that didn't work.

Seeking to avoid publicity, the hospital offered the doctors jobs in an affiliated clinic in the depressed suburb of Hartvale. Only Mona Lomasney accepted the deal, for Hartvale was the sort of place that is a springboard to nowhere. Around this time the news made the papers, which called the doctors the morphine angels. In Hartvale, Mona worked with two other doctors. The clinic took up the ground floor of a former shoe factory beneath elevated railroad tracks, and Mona lived in an apartment upstairs.

The cab driver folded the doctor's money and put it in a metal box. He opened his door and banged the bowl of his pipe on the door frame. "Listen, young people, don't be in this neighborhood after dark," he said.

Mona Lomasney came to the door of her apartment, still in pajamas. She had an angular, high-boned face that must have been amazing in her youth. Even the beautiful have their problems, among them a longer way to fall. Mona held a pair of needle-nose pliers with those slick blue grips that are so satisfying to touch. Charles could not go near needle-nose pliers without getting blood blisters on his fingers. They were the only tool he refused to use.

"My toothbrush fell down the sink," said Mona.

"This is Mona," said Dr. Palomino. "Problems follow her."

Mona laughed warily, pushing her curly brown hair over the shoulders of her striped pajamas. She looked as if she had not gotten a good night's sleep.

"*You* follow me," she said.

"This is Joan Gower Darling. We've been out walking already this morning."

"In the fog. How pretty."

"There was no fog," said Dr. Palomino.

"Let's not split hairs," said Mona. "I'm really looking forward to getting that toothbrush out."

"Let me try," said Joan. "My husband is a plumber, and I've seen what he does."

They crowded into the bathroom and stood with their backs to a clawfoot tub. The toothbrush had fallen with the bristles up, but it was too far down for the pliers to reach. The sink was small; it would hardly hold enough water to rinse your face. A thin wafer of green soap rested on one of the porcelain sides.

"Don't say I should get one of those strainer things," said Mona Lomasney. "I know that."

Joan peered into the drain.

"There is a way," she said.

"This makes me claustrophobic," said Dr. Palomino.

Mona put her hand on his arm. "There's coffee in a pan on the stove," she said. "I made it a special way I saw in a magazine, and just for you, Stephen. Because I remember what you like."

"I'll go get that now." He left them in the bathroom. Why is it, Joan thought, that a man who is sensitive and comfortable with one woman will turn officious and awkward in the presence of two? She reached behind her neck to unclasp a small silver chain that Charles had given her on some birthday. She lowered the loop of the necklace into the drain. Her fingers trembled. If she jarred the toothbrush before snaring it, it might fall down to the trap. Carefully she pulled the silver chain taut under the bristles and drew up slowly until Mona Lomasney could grab the toothbrush. They had both been holding their breath, and now they exhaled and laughed.

Joan put the necklace back on. "What's the deal with you and Stephen?"

"We lived together for two years in medical school," said Mona. "But I pulled ahead of him academically and he couldn't take it. And he thought I was seeing someone else. Which was true. We were way too young."

"I'm sorry."

"Why? You didn't do anything." Mona pressed the toothbrush into a holder on the wall. "What's the deal with *you* and Stephen?"

There was no reason not to tell the truth. "We slept together last night," said Joan. "It just happened. And now, you know, we have to spend some time together."

Dr. Palomino found three cups and poured coffee into one of them from a white metal pan with a red handle. It was exactly the sort of bright and little-used pan that a single person would have. He drank the coffee thoughtfully and called his house. His wife answered. She could be testy on the phone. Mona's kitchen smelled of coffee beans and cinnamon. The surfaces were not sticky. The doctor's wife said that she wished he had not put the storm windows on so early, since the house needed more air. She said it still smelled of smoke from the fire in the eaves. The doctor countered with his theory that if he had not told her about the fire, she would not smell anything. In other words, she said, it was all in her mind. Well, no, that was not what he meant, not exactly, only that we notice what we are prepared to notice, this is true of everyone, not just her by any means. He did it himself. It was exactly the wrong thing to say, as if he were offering her the generous gift of his own fallibility.

Mona Lomasney had a globe on her kitchen counter, and the doctor turned it idly to see if it reflected the current geography of the former Soviet Union. His wife spoke softly into the phone, offering a second "in other words" interpretation, which, like the first, suggested that he put little stock in her cognitive skills. A small purple country labeled Belarus seemed to indicate that the globe was fairly recent, but the doctor's knowledge of the eastern bloc was so sketchy that he did not know, for example, if the very term *eastern bloc* still held meaning, or why there was no *k* in *bloc*. Then his wife was saying that their son had walked in his sleep last night. He had gone up to the attic and tried to bring down his old wooden train set, mounted on plywood. He'd only managed to get it hung up in the stairwell, where she found him disoriented and angry, and this morning he had no memory of any of it. Dr. Palomino's wife loved to lay the family disturbances on him when he was out of town. The doctor pointed out that their son had not touched the train in years, and she said, *That's the point, isn't it.* He considered this remark as evidence of how his wife was better than he was, more in touch with the things one should be in touch with. But he did not really see the point made by the sleepwalking and the train.

Dr. Palomino hung up the phone, remembering the work he had put into the train set. He glued down the track segments, puttied and sanded the joints so the cars would not derail; he painted green grass, blue water, yellow roads and tracks; he worked into the small hours of the night. The boy had liked it, even though, as the doctor's wife told him later, he'd had his heart set on a bow and arrow.

"Amazing," he muttered as Joan and Mona walked into the kitchen. "How people are."

"And how is that?" said Mona.

"I don't know."

He looked at Joan with what he hoped was an expression of affection, as if to say that what had happened between them last night was an example of the mystery of human behavior.

Joan's lips were finely formed and soft-looking. He liked the way she never wore makeup. She had on a red cotton sweater and a suede skirt. Already he wanted to kiss her again. Stephen Palomino recalled a phrase he had read in a book, back when he and Mona were in college — "the most interesting woman in St. Petersburg" — and he thought that the woman in the book must have looked and acted like Joan. Maybe he was in love with her.

Mona opened the oven and took out a tray of cinnamon rolls. She put the tray on a glass table by the windows. Steam rose from the rolls as everyone pulled and cut them apart and stuffed the torn pieces into their mouths. They didn't even bother to sit down. Joan licked her knife. They were not embarrassed by their rough manners but seemed to agree that formality was not required, given their variously deficient natures. There is, the doctor thought, a well-known sort of desperation to Sunday morning. The day was too long, the newspaper too large. Also, people might be hung over from Saturday night, as he was, which never helps.

Joan asked to see the award Mona had won at Women and Infants, and Mona said she had taken a train ride to a limestone quarry one day in the spring and had thrown the Golden Pyramid into the water and watched it sink to the bottom.

"Quarries are murky as a rule," said Stephen.

"Not this one, smart boy," she said. "And all this success that everybody thinks they want, it only took me away from my work. They want you to speak here, they want you to speak there, they want you to write some introduction . . . To tell you the truth, I've never been happier than the day I walked into the clinic downstairs."

Joan moved her finger around her plate for the icing. "How come?" she said. "Because it was a chance to help people?"

"Well, there was that, but really because it was the end of my trying so hard. I mean, for the patients I try hard, but for me . . ." She waved a hand. "People thought the Golden Pyramid just fell into my lap. It's not true. I wanted it so bad I dreamed of it. I worked for it, I managed to get my name placed in consideration, I lobbied. I sought the advice of those who could help me. When you're trying to direct events, you can no longer see them for what they are."

"Which is . . . what?" said Stephen. "Because I still try."

"People fear the big downfall," said Mona. "Because they're afraid they won't be able to get up again. Because they don't think they deserve to get up again. That they're awful, and now everyone will know. But unless you fall down, you never know whether you deserve to get up. That's what the morphine scandal taught me. And I would never have found out what I had without that happening."

"This is not the American Dream," said Stephen.

"This is Mona's dream," she said.

Dr. Lomasney got dressed and took Stephen and Joan downstairs for a look at the clinic. There were lilies on the counter and pictures of other flowers on the wall. One of her partners was on duty, treating a teenager who had been shot at a friend's house. It was a minor wound, through the leg, no bones involved. The friend who had done the shooting and his father sat in the waiting room, pale, leafing through computer magazines. When the father saw new faces, he tossed his magazine aside and went to the receptionist's desk.

"Is Brice going to be all right?" he said.

Mona Lomasney nodded. "It would seem so."

The man shook hands with Mona over the counter. "What about infection? Maybe a little amoxycillin."

"Have you called the police?"

"That's what the other doctor said. So you think we should bring them into this?"

"That's the law in Hartvale," said Mona. "We'll record the accident, and they'll want to know the circumstances, whether the gun is registered and that sort of thing."

"It's just a pistol," said the man. "It isn't much of a gun. I keep it for protection. We had a clivia taken off our porch that my wife had been growing all her adult life."

"The police will want to know all these things."

"As for the gun itself . . ." He turned to his son. "Tell the doctor what we did with the gun."

The boy put down his magazine and looked at his hands. "Put it in a dumpster," he said glumly.

"That's right," said the father. "We didn't want any part of it after what it did to Brice."

"Suppose someone finds it and uses it again?" said Mona.

"That's what I said," said the boy.

"You've caused enough havoc for one day," said the father.

"I can't give legal advice," said Mona. "But you'd better get the gun if you can. And for God's sake make sure the chambers are empty."

"Well," said the man, "a clip in this case."

"What's your name?" said Mona to the boy.

"Andre."

"Come with me." She took him to a corner of the waiting room and talked to him. She kept putting her hand on his face to make him look at her.

Brice limped into the waiting room. "I've been shot," he said. "I don't expect I'll ever be the same."

His parents arrived at the clinic. They seemed too old to have a teenage son, and they walked with sagging shoulders, as if they had been pelted with stones while crossing the parking lot.

"Andre shot me," Brice told them in a tone of wonder. "I've been shot, and the bullet's in the rec room. And everything seems vivid to me now. Even these flowers, I smell them so strongly."

"I hope this doesn't ruin the friendship between our families," said Andre's father.

Brice's father screwed up his face as if he were about to

sneeze. Joan felt a pang of sympathy. Talking seemed hard for him.

"We have never liked you," he said. "Not really."

Mona's partner took the parents aside and explained how to change the dressing, and the shooter and his father headed for the door.

"Much sorrow, Brice," said his friend. "I live in shame, man."

Joan and Stephen hugged Mona and said they would let her get to her work. Mona thanked Joan for her help with the toothbrush.

"What's happened to the world?" said Joan. "What has it come to that children shoot one another and this is part of the everyday routine?"

Mona smiled sadly. "It's the same world," she said. "It's just the guns. We look everywhere for the solution. We make a show of looking. All this business of is it the movies, is it the games, is it the civilization —"

"All the sociology," said Dr. Palomino.

"It's a smokescreen," said Mona. "It's TMFG, sis."

"What's that?" said Joan.

"Think about it," said Mona.

Joan thought about it as she and Dr. Palomino left the Hartvale clinic and walked past a bridge abutment on which all manner of filthy words had been painted, and she thought about it some more as they headed across a playground toward a busy intersection where a taxi might be found. She and Stephen took a moment to sit in swings and push themselves in eddying circles as fallen leaves tumbled and scratched along the asphalt.

"Too many fucking guns," she guessed.

"That's it," said Stephen.

"Charles has guns," said Joan. "He hunts."

"He hunts in dreams."

"Maybe so."

"Oh, I don't mean Charles. It's a poem, by Alfred, Lord Tennyson. My grandfather used to read it to me. He was a big Tennyson fan. 'Like a dog, he hunts in dreams, and thou art staring at the wall, / Where the dying night-lamp flickers, and the shadows rise and fall.'"

Joan pulled herself up by the chains of the swing and stood. "He's not like a dog."

"Of course not," said the doctor. "Listen. Don't think of what's happened. Don't dwell on it. We're going back home. Are you on the four o'clock flight?"

"No."

"Meet me tomorrow in Stone City."

"I don't know. I have a lot to do."

"We could have lunch," he said. "There's a Marvin Cone show at the museum. You would like his paintings."

"I'll try."

A church stood at the intersection, and she remembered that it was Sunday and she had not gone to church. She never missed and would not miss on this day of days, with her damp and incriminating swimsuit folded over the curtain rod of the Astrid Hotel. So Stephen took a taxi alone and Joan went into the church, where the liturgy was proceeding. She moved sideways into an aisle and picked up the *Book of Common Prayer* — only for something to hold on to, because she knew the responses by heart. She did not hope for revelation, as once she would have. For years Joan had expected a bolt out of the blue, something new and alarming that would descend, giving shape to her life. This is why she had been an actress, why she had been a proselyte, why she had studied the stars. It was deliverance she had been looking for in the churches and on the stages and in the sky, and she no longer thought it would come simply. If she could tell someone all that was in her mind, maybe she could make a start, but this was not a church that featured confession. After the service, she approached the minister anyway. He said to give him fifteen minutes and then meet him in his office in the basement. She found him talking on the telephone.

"No. That's fine. That's fine. In fact it's good," he said. "I'm not going. I have no intention. Who said so? If I wanted to go, believe me, I would have been there and back."

The room had a musty and tomblike smell that made it hard for Joan to breathe, let alone explain her guilt and confusion. She put her hands on the minister's desk and leaned on it for a moment.

He hung up the phone.

"I don't know how to begin," said Joan.

"Don't," he said. "I'm sorry, I have to go. I'm very sorry."

11 · Micah

COLETTE GOT UP EARLY and fried doughnuts in an electric pan. Micah sat in a chair at the table, numb with sleep. What had he dreamed? He knew the shadows of it but not what made the shadows. Colette moved around the kitchen, talking quietly to herself. She had no idea of his late wandering, because when he got back to her house, the door was not locked. He had been turning the knob the wrong way, that was all.

Instead of putting the doughnuts on a plate, Colette laid them in a shoebox lined with wax paper. Then she took Micah back to his house in her car, an old Chevy Nova with a forest-green litter bag hanging from the tuning knob of the radio. She explained that she would be going on to Spillville, to see the world-famous Bily clocks and the memorial to the composer Antonín Dvořák. She had been planning this trip for some time.

Micah carried the shoebox into the house. He and his father ate the warm, jagged doughnuts and said very little. There was a deep scratch on Charles's nose.

"What did you do?" said Micah.

"Bumped myself."

"On what?"

"A coat hanger."

Later on, the farmer named Skel who had been at the auction barn came by to drop off a book about raising goats. Lyris was still asleep, so Skel gave the book to Charles and Micah.

"As I say, I don't recommend them as a rule," said Skel. "They're not much of a cash animal, and I don't like the way they look at you."

"Is that right," said Charles absently. The book was called *Modern Goat Husbandry,* and like many books with *modern* in the title, it was old, with a woven binding of dark orange.

"It always seemed to me they were expecting something," Skel explained. "Whereas a cow, feed *it* and hell, you're the best friend it ever had. A hog, of course, is a different story. I don't say a hog is friendly, far from it. But once they understand they can't kill you, they become indifferent. Why, I remember one cold day in January —"

"What do you feed a goat?" said Charles. "We got some alfalfa yesterday. Are we on the right track?"

"We had a mix," said Skel. "We give ours a mix until we decided to let them go."

"You let them go?" said Micah. He pictured Skel's goats traipsing about the countryside.

"What I mean is we sold them."

A woman got out of Skel's car, a glossy white purse under her arm. "We have to go, Skel."

"What'd we feed our goats, Lucy?" said Skel. "What was that mix?"

"What you been giving 'em?" said Lucy.

"Alfalfa," said Micah.

"We didn't do that," said Skel. "But it is done."

Lucy nodded. She had a rugged face that made her look as if she could do anything. "Some go that route. What we did was shake up one part oats, one part Ringmaster Show Lamb, one part black sunflower seeds, and then sometimes a little nutmeg."

Many buckets, and one with black sunflower seeds . . . The future was taking shape before Micah's eyes, and it was good.

"And for cream, good news there, don't bother with a separator," said Skel. "Just put the milk in a big open jar in the refrigerator and leave it overnight."

Micah and Charles stood in the yard and watched the farmers drive off in a silver Lincoln Town Car. "Here," said Charles, handing Micah the goat book.

Micah wished that Joan were there to read to him. They had an early-morning ritual in which they would lie in Joan and Charles's bed and Joan would hold a book in her left hand while draping her right arm over his shoulders. "Arm position," Micah would say, and she would provide it, reading in her quiet, steady voice, Micah turning the pages. Charles would read aloud, but he could not resist adding sarcastic remarks, and when he got tired of a story, he would say, "And so they all moved away. The end."

"When's Mom coming home?" said Micah.

"Late afternoon, early evening."

Micah carried his sleeping bag into the yard, unzipped it, and spread it under the willow tree. The light was more blue than yellow. He thought it important to notice the way the light was. It fell on the side of the birch trunk, which had bright bark and black scars. When the winter ice came, the birch would bend over the driveway so that its branches scratched the roof of Charles's van, and Charles would remind himself to cut it down, but he never did. Micah pushed his shoes off with his toes and lay stocking-footed and holding *Modern Goat Husbandry* by Lloyd Mumquill between his face and the light. He liked the coolness of the breeze, because the house always seemed too cold or too hot, and this morning it had been too hot. He had had trouble breathing and felt a cold coming on, as his mother would say.

On the left-hand page opposite the title was a drawing of a goat with a comical animated face and the words *Help Me!* printed above its head. This made the book seem simple, but it was not. Micah read the introduction:

The average goat operation in this country clears a net of five to six percent. If this book could have the wondrous yet at the same time modest effect of reducing costs by one percent per hundredweight per annum while simultaneously increasing monthly dairy output by as little as nine ounces per mature nanny (see Appendix C), these figures would rise smartly, with seven percent becoming the floor and eleven percent the ceiling of our new and attractively remodeled "house." No steward of *C. hircus* in this nation could resist an invitation to such a dwelling, and yet many prefer to stumble on in the wilds of blameless ignorance of certain economies. Now I want to introduce a phrase you will encounter with some frequency in these pages. *It Does Not Have to Be So!* Remember this and apply it throughout your daily chores and you will have learned all I have to teach. "Then tell me why, Mumquill," you may say. "Tell me why I should read on." This is a fair question. Perhaps you have examined other books pertaining to goat management and found them wanting. Lord knows I have. Many of these august publications look forward to a day when the pendulum of public opinion will swing from that virtual poison known as cow's "milk" (the quote marks indicating my belief that cow's milk is not milk at all but rather some dyspeptic and Vitamin A–deficient liquid of indeterminate nature, a danger to infants and old-timers alike, the Alpha and Omega of family living). Until that great changeful day, these utopian tracts suggest, the goat farmer is doomed to the here-a-penny-there-a-penny subsistence with which many of us are sadly familiar. Thus the solutions to our difficulties lie outside ourselves. Start a local production board! Catch the ear of a newspaperman! And if we all

set to proselytizing from coast to coast, then slowly, impercepti-
bly, rich rewards will accrue, et cetera, if not to the present gen-
eration, then to its luckier heirs in some distant day. This approach, championed most prominently by Marilyn Faber in
Goat and Man, which has seen an impressive if unfortunate six
printings, frankly nauseates me. Moreover, *It Does Not Have to
Be So!*

This is as far as Micah got, and that he did so was a testament
to his perseverance. In order to keep going he had replaced the
words he did not understand with other words that started the
same way, which resulted in sentences that made no sense. If
Joan were here, he thought, he would have her read not this
book but some other book — *The Railway Children,* with the
wrongly accused and absent father.

Micah lay on his back looking at the sky. The bending yellow reeds of the willow moved slowly against the blue. He
sneezed, swiped the back of his arm across his nose, rose from
the sleeping bag, and walked around behind the house. He
batted the streamers of moss that spilled from the clotted eaves
and grabbed a garbage-can lid to deflect the goat's charges.
The goat, however, did not want to fight. She lay in the sun,
gazing up at Micah. There were mounds of manure here and
there on the grass — perfect bearings of dark and shiny green,
as if the alfalfa had gone through the goat without changing.

Micah fetched a hairbrush from the house and went to
work on the goat's red coat. Dusty hanks of hair came off on
the bristles. Sometimes the goat tried to bite, but not seriously.
Micah patted the bony crest of her head with one hand while
brushing with the other.

The goat struggled up on its hard-shelled feet, as if to signal
the arrival of an intruder. It was Micah's Uncle Jerry, who said,
"Oh, God."

"That's right," said Micah. "We got her yesterday."

"You want to go to a show?"

Having resented Jerry ever since he had cut down his tent, Micah said nothing.

"You don't even know what it's about."

"Tent wrecker," said Micah.

"Why'd you get a goat?"

"Lyris's going to raise it for 4-H. But it's half mine."

"You'll rue the day."

"It does not have to be so," said Micah.

Jerry rattled a newspaper in his hands and folded it twice. "Look here," he said. "If this doesn't interest you, then you're no relation of mine."

"Meet Gabriel Rain and His Huskies Monk & Tandy," said the advertisement. The photograph showed a man standing between two proud dogs. The animals sat alert and open-mouthed and had thick silvery ruffs. "Melodeon Theater."

The goat ripped the newspaper from Jerry's hands and began tearing it up.

"Hey," said Jerry. "Give that back."

"She doesn't listen to anyone," said Micah. He picked up a shred of paper. "Look how small she makes it."

Micah had been to the Melodeon in Morrisville once before. He and Charles and Joan had gone to see an old movie called *Charlie the Lonesome Cougar,* but they missed the first twenty minutes, and when they tried to stay for the beginning of the next show the usher said they couldn't. Charles argued for a long time, but when they were halfway home he seemed to have forgotten all about it. That night they ate at a fish fry in a tavern in Chesley. Charles surprised Joan and Micah by going around to all the booths and drinking water from the glasses of the other customers. The people didn't like it, anyone could tell, but most let him do what he wanted. Micah and Joan looked at each other and laughed with their mouths if not with their eyes. Micah thought that Charles was like the cougar in the movie, in that those who did not know him were afraid of him and those who did know him were keenly aware of this general fear without having any solution.

Now a horde of kids milled and shouted outside the Melodeon, and Jerry and Micah were carried along by the crowd. Someone shoved Micah hard in the small of the back, and he turned on a larger and older boy. Charles had advised him to go for the knees in a fight, but when Micah pictured the pale and lumpy knees of the bully, he could not do it. This was why he would never be a good fighter. He always thought of the other person, and by then he was lost. A tedious shirt fight ensued. Jerry separated the two boys and asked if this was any way to carry on.

At that moment a long convertible pulled up in front of the theater. It was driven by Gabriel Rain, whom everyone recognized from the picture in the newspaper. The dogs, Monk and Tandy, sat stoically on either side of the back seat.

"This is nothing new to them," Jerry commented. "They've seen it all a thousand times."

Gabriel Rain stepped from the car holding the propeller of an airplane. What this signified no one could say, but dozens of kids rushed him while the dogs cast their eyes about uneasily.

"See there," Jerry said into Micah's ear. "A normal dog, in this situation you would have a problem."

"Get back," said Gabriel Rain. "Get back, I say." The wave of children broke and subsided, and the dog trainer raised the propeller over his head. "Now that you've all had a chance to see the movie, I thought —"

"What movie?" screamed several children at once.

"We ain't *seen* any movie!" said the one who had pushed Micah, in that triumphant and slightly hysterical voice some children employ when an adult has made a big obvious error.

The owner of the theater stepped forward to deal with the

misunderstanding. He twisted his hands while speaking quietly to Gabriel Rain, who tossed the propeller across the front seat of the car and listened impatiently. A funeral procession moved past, the slow black hearse followed by a line of clean cars with their headlights on. This quieted the crowd for a while, and the mourners looked at the dogs.

"Well, we *haven't* seen no movie," said Micah's adversary.

Gabriel Rain removed his cowboy hat and held it over his heart. But once the last car had bumped over the railroad tracks, he threw the hat on the pavement and began berating the theater owner.

"Did you think I was going to be here all day?" he said. He bent to retrieve the hat, and a pair of sunglasses fell from the pocket of his jacket. "That's not in the contract, sir, which you signed." He took a piece of paper from the dashboard of the car and unfolded it. "It specifically says," he said, and then he went into the details of the contract, which no one cared about.

The theater owner and Gabriel Rain reduced their argument to angry whispers. It cheered Micah to see that the owner was not going quietly but had adopted a pretty insistent tone himself. The two men hissed and pointed at each other with their forefingers held close to their chests, as if they could hide their animosity from the crowd. Then one of the dogs barked, and Gabriel Rain stopped talking.

"It's like the dogs have trained him," said Jerry.

Micah stepped forward to rescue Gabriel Rain's sunglasses from the gutter. He breathed on the lenses, polished them with his shirttail, and handed the glasses to the showman.

"Thank you," said Gabriel Rain. "It has come to my attention, everyone, that you have *not* seen the movie. Thus my visual aid" — he indicated the propeller on the seat of the car — "has perhaps caused nothing but confusion. Well, go in. Go in and see the movie. That's what you've paid for, or are about to, and you won't be disappointed. After the movie, there will be a demonstration in which Monk and Tandy will perform live some of the amazing stunts that you are about to witness on the screen, including the climbing of stepladders and so forth."

Micah liked the movie, a black-and-white thriller in which the dogs were the real stars. The role of Gabriel Rain, whom no one had ever heard of apart from the advertisement in the newspaper, was played by someone else, who was equally unfamiliar. The story went like this: A doctor who flew his own plane was trying to transport vital medicine to an orphanage on a mountain. The villain wanted to stop the shipment so the orphanage would close and he could buy its land, under which lay zinc deposits, according to the map that he took pleasure in rolling out with a great rustling sound on tables, car hoods, and other flat surfaces. Gabriel Rain and his dogs enlisted on the side of the doctor, and there were many interesting shots of the dogs riding in the doctor's plane with mountains and trees in the background. At one point the villain removed the propeller from the plane and buried it, but Monk and Tandy pawed it up from the ground and took turns carrying it back to the airport.

So that's where the propeller came in.

Micah sat with his feet up on the seat and his arms wrapped around his knees, so engrossed in the film that it took him some time to notice what the usher was doing. She delivered food and drinks to Jerry and Micah. She also came and sat with them sometimes, and it was not long before Micah realized it was Lyris's friend Octavia Perry.

"*Micah,*" she said, as if his name were something to make fun of.

"*Taffy,*" he responded, but his show of disgust was muted and perfunctory, since the bad guy was at that moment training the telescopic sight of a rifle on Monk the husky.

When Micah looked over to share his enthusiasm with Jerry and Taffy, he could see that Taffy was upset, and might even have been crying. She opened her mouth wide and pressed the heels of her hands to her face. Micah did not believe that she was worried about the huskies or the fate of the hilltop orphans. Then Jerry said he and Octavia were going for a walk. They moved off down the aisle toward the looming screen and out the door where EXIT glowed in red letters.

Micah met Jerry and Octavia in front of the Melodeon after the movie. Gabriel Rain and the dogs were gone. Micah had not really expected to see them again. The wind had picked up, and the sky seemed deep and vivid after the darkness of the theater. Octavia was smiling, which made Micah glad, for although he disliked her, he did not want to see anyone sad. Some of the parents who had brought their kids to the show were trying to work up a head of steam over the showman's defection, but their anger was hard to sustain.

Jerry treated Taffy and Micah to ice cream at Birdsall's, and Micah tried to send a subtle hint to Taffy about his uncle's age by asking Jerry to tell what it had been like in South Korea when he was stationed there. Jerry had spent three years in the late seventies working as an electrician for armed forces television in the city of Seoul. He said he remembered exactly where he was when they got the word that President Park had been assassinated. He'd been in the apartment of a friend of his, and they'd been listening to a record by Doug Sahm. And he remembered the song that had been playing, "(Is Anybody Going to) San Antone." Octavia looked at him as if she were going to jump across the table and take *him* to San Antone. Like Micah, she would not have known President Park or Doug Sahm from a box of apples, and yet Micah's question had done just the opposite of what he had hoped it might do.

12 · Charles

CHARLES SEEMED TO RECALL some rule against staining over paint, but he had stain and he didn't have paint, and he chalked up the rule to paint store propaganda. He enjoyed the fumes and the wood grain and the even strokes required to stain the barn doors. He came up with thoughts that began profoundly but for which he had no ending: *In this world you have two choices. No, in this world you have three choices.* He dipped the brush into green stain and sloughed off the excess by dragging the bristles over the clotted rim. *In a restaurant you may have five choices, but in this world you don't get that many.*

Micah came home from the dog show, interrupting this train of thought, which Charles knew was useless yet found somehow engaging. Wound up, the boy bounced around relaying the events of his afternoon at the theater, most of which served as prelude, in his telling, to his heroic retrieval of the dog trainer's sunglasses from the street. Then Jerry came over to the barn and Micah ran around the back yard calling "Yai, yai, yai" in a strangled voice. This was something he was compelled to do from time to time to burn off energy.

The goat, which Charles had untied to see if it would stay

around when it did not have to, tripped after the boy; it really seemed to understand the concept of play.

"Got another brush?" said Jerry.

Charles found one in a can in the barn. He freed it from a bottom-dwelling pad of congealed turpentine and bent the bristles back and forth, so that flakes of old paint fell on the cuffs of his shirt. The half-brothers worked in silence as the shadows of the trees stretched toward them.

Finally Jerry spoke. "You know, I've never had very much in the way of . . ."

Love or money would have been Charles's guess, but he only nodded his head thoughtfully.

"Well, what?" said Jerry. "Companionship."

"This is not the postman's way," said Charles. "You guys kind of keep to yourselves, until one day some little thing happens and you go off like a roman candle."

"I expect more from you," said Jerry.

"And so do I," said Charles. "So do I. Sometimes I think, Well, I'm just a crumb and so be it. But in this case, I take it back. This is about Octavia, isn't it? Must be."

"It's about Octavia," said Jerry.

"All the forces of the world are lined up against you," said Charles. "Knowing that, if you still — or if she, because I think she's the one who has to . . . Ah, but I don't know, Jerry, it's just too —"

"Unconventional," said Jerry.

"It is that." Charles slapped a brush full of stain onto the door and smoothed it up and down. "She's young," he said. "She's real young."

"Past the age of consent."

"What is that?"

"Sixteen, isn't it?"

"Did they raise it when they raised the drinking age?"

"I don't know. I never heard that."

"You'd better check."

"*You've* never been conventional," said Jerry. But in this approach he was playing a losing hand.

"I've got the kids," said Charles.

"Pure luck."

"It is luck. What else would it be? And Joan."

"You took a while to marry her."

"Nevertheless. We went to a justice of the peace. And I've been *divorced*. What could be more conventional than that? And there's the house."

He looked around the yard. The goat was carrying the lid of the garbage can like a retriever with a Frisbee. All right, forget the goat as an example. He gestured toward the barn.

"I don't see the relevance of the barn," said Jerry.

Charles shrugged. "Evidence of conventionality."

"Which is about to fall down."

"There are cracks in the foundation."

"And for that matter, I have a house and a shed."

"This is true." Having said that, Charles had to take a break, for it was a phrase his first wife, Louise, had often used. Thinking of the divorce, he had slipped into her mode of speaking. He and Jerry sat down in the grass.

"You have stain on your eyebrow," said Jerry.

Charles rubbed the back of his forearm across his brow.

"You're just pushing it around."

"Look," said Charles, "what you have to do is ask yourself what is in Octavia's best interest. You could ask *her*, but that begs the question of whether she can make a reasoned judgment, which I'm not sure she can. Now is one thing. Think when she's forty and you're some decrepit thing she has to wheel around in a cart."

"I have thought of that," said Jerry. "What if it was only a couple years. We sing in the sunshine, she gets her mind together, goes off to college. I wouldn't complain . . . I'd make that trade in a heartbeat."

"Why?"

"I get a kick out of her. I like her. Who can say?"

"She wouldn't be pregnant."

"No."

"She has parents."

"They don't talk."

"To each other or to her?"

"To anyone, from what she tells me."

"What if they put a contract out on your life? Who are they again?"

"Teachers."

"Right," said Charles. "That might work in your favor, and it might not."

He went into the kitchen and got two bottles of Falstaff. On the way back he remembered that he wanted to ask whether Octavia would get a G.E.D., just because it sounded like the kind of star-crossed plan that would inevitably call for a G.E.D. somewhere along the line. Perhaps Jerry and Octavia could get their diplomas together, then go to the sock hop.

Charles gave Jerry a beer. He did not know what to tell his older brother. Probably Jerry would do whatever he wanted anyway.

Colette looked at clocks made of walnut, butternut, maple, and oak in the building in which the composer Dvořák once stayed. She especially liked the apostle clock and the Festina church clock, even though she was an agnostic. Dvořák was said to have worked on his "American Quartette" here. Still, Colette could not get the "Ring-Around-the-Rosie Rag" out of her head. A brochure said that the Bily brothers, who had made the clocks, "employed the idle hours of long winter days and evenings with their skills of woodcarving." The other tourists included a couple with a little girl who walked around in circles, eating small candy bars and dropping the wrappers on the floor. Later Colette saw the couple crossing the street, the father holding the sleeping child in both arms.

This reminded Colette of the time Charles almost died. He and Jerry had been roughhousing and Tiny had hit his head on the corner of a coffee table. They were just kids. Colette held the back of an ashtray to Tiny's mouth, and no cloud formed on the glass. They had no phone, so she gathered him up in her arms, just as this man now held his sleeping daughter, and carried him out the door. Jerry and Bebe followed, making small sounds of suppressed hysteria. Sunlight fell around them, as though nothing was wrong.

Colette raised her ashen son to the air.

There was no one on the road, and they didn't have a car. The lilac bush loomed like death's messenger at the end of their path. The heavy boy began to slip, and she hoisted her arms to renew her purchase. It was this little bump, gathering and lifting, that started him breathing again. He tossed his head and wheezed, and she laid him on the picnic table amid a swarm of mourning cloak butterflies that had been hovering over something sweet on the boards.

After that she felt for many years that Charles had been spared in order to achieve things. Now she wondered what obstacle had kept him from them. The same could be asked vis-à-vis Jerry. If only they'd had woodcarving skills to employ in their idle hours, they might have something to show for themselves. Bebe had done all right, in far-off California. She sometimes sent pictures of her friends by her swimming pool.

Maybe time was the enemy, thought Colette. The Bily brothers never thought so, making all those clocks. But where did time take them? To St. Wenceslaus Cemetery, where, if she hurried, she might see their graves before the light was gone.

The volunteer fire department met every night of the week, but attendance was optional. Given this congenial arrangement, the place often had the feel of a nightclub with trucks. Tonight a new volunteer would be initiated, and when Jerry arrived the lights were low and the running boards of the ladder truck were lined with burning candles. The initiate was a young man barely out of community college. He was no one Jerry knew. The fire chief insisted on the use of the sound system, for its eerie, echoing effects, and Jerry took his place behind the graphic equalizer. He slid the level bars randomly up and back while the fire chief recited a poem to test the speakers.

"'Last night, she said, a star did fall / From heaven's ceaseless costume ball. / It lit the night but for a minute, / With gold and blue and silver in it, / My rent, she said, is due tomorrow / But I can only pay in sorrow.' How's that?" said the fire chief. He wore a blue flannel shirt, leaned on a cane, and scratched the wiry beard he had grown for the town's centennial.

"I don't get it," said Jerry.

The newcomer was brought forth in full gear: yellow boots, a dun suit circled about the calves and biceps with reflective yellow, a cylinder of compressed air, a red helmet, a breathing apparatus and face mask that suggested space travel. On his chest he wore a round and fluted pressure regulator. He carried a box-end hydrant wrench, and as he staggered into place the other firefighters remembered how disorienting that first time on oxygen had been.

The fire chief read the induction speech slowly, without emphasis. He wanted to stir emotion with the words, not with a dramatic tone. There were references to Prometheus, to the chemist Antoine Lavoisier, who discovered oxygen's role in fire, to the virgins who had tended the fires of the Temple of

Vesta. As a speech, it was all over the place. Like the poem, it had been written by the fire chief in his spare time.

"And when it's cold," the chief recited, "and when it's late, and the snow lies roundabout, deep and crisp and even — when you least want the siren to sound — sound it does, oh yes, its mournful cry piercing the night at three A.M. or three-thirty . . ."

The sergeant at arms helped the subject out of his heavy gear, and the ladder master uncorked a bottle of grappa and poured one part liquor and two parts coffee into a wooden bowl known as the friendship cup. Meanwhile the new fireman walked beside the ladder truck, leaning down to pinch out the candles on the runner. As each was extinguished, the firefighters shouted "Hurrah," according to custom. This was Jerry's least favorite part of the induction ceremony, few crowds being as self-conscious as the one obliged to shout "Hurrah." He would have preferred something less painfully traditional, such as Micah's "Yai, yai, yai." Then came the drinking from the friendship cup. This had been outfitted with a number of straws emerging from holes in the wood.

Jerry was one of the last men to take a drink. He and Leo Miner held the bowl and drew on the straws. Leo worked at the door factory. He had long hair, and deep crevices bracketed his mouth.

"Do you have a niece named Lila?" asked Leo as he set the friendship cup on a card table.

"Lyris?"

"Yeah . . . *Lyris.*"

"Shirttail relation. My brother's daughter, or half-daughter, I guess you'd say."

Leo laughed softly and shook his head. "So hard just to keep *track* of people, it seems like, these days."

"What about her?"

"Well, it ain't none of my business, but . . ." he began, motioning Jerry away from the table. They went over and sat on the front bumper of the water truck. Leo polished the chrome intake cap with his handkerchief. "I run into her over in Martins Woods last night," he said. "This Follard . . . You know William Follard, they call him Billy sometimes."

"Yeah."

"But you know him."

"Not to say hello, but yeah."

"Well, and I couldn't say the whys and wherefores of it, but evidently —" And here his voice grew quiet, and he bent low, forearms on knees, looking not at Jerry but at the floor, as if to suggest it was all in confidence and he would deny saying it if questioned. "'Parently this Follard, from what I understand, and again, none of this comes firsthand, but if you asked me if it sounded true, I would have to say it did."

"Christ, just say it," said Jerry, who had adopted the folded posture of his informant.

"That he threw her, threw Lyris —"

"Follard did."

"Yes, off the bridge," said Leo. "And now, I'm assuming this would've have been the second of the ones they call Four Bridges. I found her in Sprague Heileman's cabin, up off the North Pin River."

"What would he do that for?"

"They disagreed," said Leo. "And what about I will leave to your imagination. Because she didn't say. She'd been in the water. That much I do know."

"So she — let me understand — Lyris was . . . well, she got to the cabin somehow."

"Walked, I guess. And she's Tiny's kid?"

"Yeah," said Jerry, adding, "Charles," as if Joan were there to correct them.

"He isn't going to like this."

"No, he is not."

"There again, maybe he knows."

Jerry sat back and rested his arm on the headlight of the truck. He and Leo breathed a little sigh of relief at having moved from the information itself to the logistics of its distribution. "Well, I just came from there, couple hours ago, and if he does, he didn't say so."

"But then, you wouldn't. A person might not."

"We're pretty open that way."

"The thing is, I wouldn't have told you," said Leo. "That's what kills me. I really don't think I would have, if it hadn't been that it was Follard. Because to me, and I only speak for myself, a guy like that, with the —"

"History."

"History, reputation, there are many names for it. A guy like that."

"Oh, I know it."

"I heard that one time Follard beat somebody so bad that the next time the person saw him, you know, across the street or however it went, his nose started bleeding on the spot — spontaneously."

"Yeah?"

"And if you let something slide . . ."

"You can't let it slide."

The doors of the water truck opened, the bumper fell as men climbed into the cab, the headlights came on. Jerry and Leo got up and moved out of the way. Some of the firefighters were taking the new kid out for a spin around town. The truck pulled out of the barn with men hanging on to the rails in their rain gear. Jerry had another drink from the friendship cup and went upstairs. He took out his keys and opened the office door. This was the chief's room, where he wrote his poetry. Jerry stood with his hand on the telephone. No one wanted to bear bad news to Charles. But what choice did Jerry have? His brother's family was so isolated out there, on that flat road in that open country, not counting the company they gave each other.

He sat down in a green leather chair with brass studs along the arms. The chair must have cost three hundred or more. He thought it odd that although the town was virtually deserted, the volunteer fire department had the latest of all good things. A siren sounded from the far end of town. There was no fire, they were just fooling around with the truck. The kid would be having a good time, with no inkling of the misery and danger he would encounter at fires. Jerry remembered an apartment fire in which a finch had died of smoke inhalation in its cage. He had drawn the unhappy job of carrying the cage out of the building and delivering it to the woman whose bird it was. The finch sat motionless on the perch, head bent and eyes closed.

"Will it be all right?" she asked him.

"It's hard to say," said Jerry.

This was a small example — there were many worse ones he could think of — and yet it stayed with him. And he thought he had been cowardly in that moment, not to tell her the truth.

Charles hung up the phone. He had assumed it would be Joan, who should have been long home by now. Supper was over, dishes piled in the sink. He walked through the house, calling for Lyris to come down. She met him on the landing with a blanket around her shoulders. He told her that he had to go out and that she would be in charge of Micah until he got back. The girl's eyes searched his face. She knew that trouble had come, but not from which direction. Was it about Joan? she asked. Charles said it was not; she would be rolling up at any minute.

"Take care of your brother," he said.

The night was cold and rainy. He hoped that the stained

doors would not streak. The wipers on the van barely skimmed the windshield, and the headlights of oncoming traffic slid and surged on the watery glass. He drove up to Stone City and parked in the driveway of Follard's house. Then, on second thought, he backed the van into the street and pulled onto the grass, stopping short of the front door, where a porch light was on.

He knocked. "Come in," said a small reed of a voice.

He opened the door and stepped into a hallway. The wallpaper was purple, dark, printed with grapes. There wasn't much light. Incense burned in a porcelain cup on a table. It took him a minute to see into the gloom, but eventually he made out the woman who had invited him in. She was a little old thing wearing an Iowa State sweatshirt.

"I'm looking for William Follard," said Charles.

"Is something wrong?" she said, busy polishing the handle of a fireplace poker. "I'm his aunt. I live next door. If it's about a jackhammer, I can tell you that *I've* never seen it, and I think it would be a very tricky thing to hide."

"It would be," said Charles. "But I didn't come for a jackhammer. William put in an application, and it looks like I'm hiring."

She worked the fireplace tool over with a cloth. "What sort of work? He has a job."

"I'm a plumber," said Charles. He opened the front door. "This is my van."

"You mustn't drive on Billy's yard."

"I'll only be a minute," said Charles.

She wrapped her fingers around the banister and called up the stairs. "Billy," she said. "Billy, come down."

Something knocked against the floor above. Then Charles heard Follard's voice, but he could not get what he was saying.

"There's a man here," said the aunt. "There's a plumber.

Come down. He's in the house right now. It's something about a job."

"I didn't call a plumber," said Follard.

She smiled patiently. "Come down and talk to him. Don't stand up there all night long."

The aunt looked at Charles. "Billy's a bachelor, and he never takes time to think of the hospitality that makes a house a home. I've been like a mother to him. That's what my friends tell me. That I mother him and mother him, try to do it all, never taking time to think of myself."

"Do you live here?"

"Oh my, no. I live next door."

Charles took the fireplace tool from the woman and urged her to leave, as the business he had to talk over with William would be of no interest to anyone but William and himself.

"Go on home and have yourself a nightcap," he said, and nodded, as if it were her thought instead of his.

She put on a belted wool coat and left reluctantly. The door closed and opened, and she peeked in. "Tell him I'm leaving."

"Follard," Charles yelled. "Your aunt is leaving now."

When she was gone, Charles locked the door. He threw the poker down a stairwell to the cellar.

"Who are you?" said Follard, ambling down the steps, buttoning a white shirt. He was tall but with no weight to speak of.

"My name is Tiny Darling. I'm Lyris's father and I know what happened last night."

"I don't know what you're talking about."

"Then it will all come as a great mystery to you."

"Get out of here, old-timer," said Follard. His eyes seemed drowsy and aimless. "Get out before I hurt you."

Follard jumped the banister and came sailing down. Charles turned his back and Follard landed on it. Charles was struck less by the impact than by the strangeness of the tactic. When you were on someone's back, you had very little control of the field. But if this was his approach, then let it be. Follard clamped an arm around Charles's windpipe and dug his fingers into Charles's eyes. Charles could have fought this kid blind, he really thought so. Yet he was having trouble breathing, and felt a sharpness in his neck. He crouched and staggered, gripping Follard's arms as if they were a muffler that he was wearing on a winter's day. Follard held on tight, until Charles could no longer think clearly. Fragments of memory ran through his mind in no order he could understand. This couldn't go on much longer. Through a film of tears, Charles saw the newel post. He rolled his shoulders and swung Follard into the column. Then he stepped into the front room and dropped the young man on the floor.

"My ribs," said Follard.

"I'll bet they hurt."

Charles set the toe of his boot on Follard's sternum and put a little weight there. Now it was Follard who couldn't breathe.

"If you ever . . ." Charles began. "But why put limits on it? You know what I mean."

Charles left the house and walked through the rain to his van. He clasped his hands around his neck, turned his head from side to side. Something was stuck in there. He removed it, looked at it in the light: a jackknife with a pheasant on it. Charles wiped the blade on his coat, closed the knife, and put it in his pocket. Behind the wheel again, he pushed a blue handkerchief down between his collar and the wound. Heart racing, he lowered his forehead to the steering wheel. He was not hurt much. Fighting always did this to him.

ᗌ Monday

13 · Joan

JOAN SEEMED to be swimming, rather than running, away from home. It was Monday morning, and she was in the pool of the Astrid Hotel once again, watching her reflection move across the ceiling of blue mirrors. She was glad the doctor had gone home. It made everything simpler. Long ago, she had walked from door to door, offering religion to all those who would listen. She remembered traveling dusty roads, white Bible in her hands, red-winged blackbirds flitting from post to post. Like everyone, she wanted something back that she used to have, and it was nowhere to be found.

Her family would wait for her. Joan was operating under the common illusion that the life of those she knew became circular in her absence. Micah would orbit the yard and fall off his bike; Lyris would lie in the grass eating raw cauliflower; Charles would fix something in such a way that it would need fixing again soon. And one day she would return to them, settled and strong, herself again. It is easy to feel resilient in a swimming pool, because your natural buoyancy is all that keeps you from sinking.

The telephone was ringing when she returned to her room. It was one of those weightless hotel phones, so overburdened with lights and information that it seemed to have a life of its own. To pick up the receiver would be an unwarranted intrusion. She lay on the bed, listening to the sound the phone made, an electronic bird call that would fool no birds. It was as if an accident were happening before her eyes and she could not raise a hand.

The phone stopped ringing. Joan got dressed, put her extra clothes in a drawstring plastic bag, and called the laundry department. A woman said she would send someone up. It was seven-thirty. Micah and Lyris would be getting ready for school, brushing their teeth, tying their shoes.

Joan called Charles to say she would come home in the spring. She told him she needed time to think. She had seen movies and TV shows in which this request, once made, was routinely granted. Charles, though, being neither movie star nor concerned TV husband, gave her no time to think.

"The spring?" he said. "What is it, Joan? What has happened? Did you go and find someone new?"

"No," she said. "Not really. Not in the way you mean. Have I been unfaithful? Yes. Have you? Don't tell me you haven't. But this has to do with us and not with anyone else. You stopped believing in me, Charles. You put me off to the side, where I became another person."

"Oh, Joan."

"Speak into the phone, honey."

"That doesn't sound like me."

"Let me go, just for a while, let me go."

"When were you with this man? Are you with him now?"

"He's gone. I'm sorry if it hurts."

"Do you know what I was doing last night? Taking a knife out of my neck."

"That is just how it feels," she said. "As if a knife has been removed. I love you, Charles. I always will, in my heart. Just please tell Micah and Lyris I will be home in the spring."

"Where are you going?" he said. "Where will you be?"

"I don't know yet," she said. "Goodbye."

In a little while there was a knock at the door. Joan gave her clothes to a young porter, who waited for a tip. Getting none, he shrugged and walked off.

"Wait," called Joan. She met the porter in the hall and gave him two dollars.

"Do I seem old to you?" she said.

"To me? No."

"Well, how old do I seem? Take a wild guess. Don't worry about my feelings."

"Thirty-two," said the porter, and Joan felt better, although the figure sounded rehearsed, as if it had been suggested in the hotel handbook. "When will you want them back?"

"Want what back?"

"Your things."

"I don't," she said. "Clean them, charge it to my room, and after that I don't care what happens to them."

"Why not throw them away?" said the porter.

"Good idea."

"Look, miss —"

"I don't care about the clothes. Can't you see that?"

She left the hotel with her suitcase in her hand. There was almost nothing in it, but she did not want to be the sort of woman who begins a new life without a suitcase.

The streets that had been empty yesterday were now very busy. Everyone had somewhere to go, and so did she, although she did not know where. Charles would tell the children, and there would be no going back now. He would tell them at the first chance, and with bitterness. If only she had kept Lyris as an infant instead of having her handed back so late, things would have been different. Yet they all might wait for her. Micah would; he was true-blue. And spring was not far away. It would be winter and then it would be spring. She wondered if she would keep her promise. It was easier to say "I'll be home in the spring" than it was to say "I won't be coming home."

She needed someone to talk to. The person she and Dr. Palomino had seen in the sleeping bag was not in front of the bakery but down the street. He sat with his back to a fence, drinking an orange drink, his long gray hair falling over his shoulders. Long-haired people always struck Joan as wise. She walked up and down the block, crossing and recrossing his territory, working up the nerve to speak.

"Do you mind if I sit down?" she said.

"No," he said.

She sat down beside him. They said nothing for five minutes.

"Don't you want to know what I'm doing, with my suitcase?" said Joan.

"Oh, tell me."

"I'm leaving my family."

"Don't."

"I have to," said Joan. She opened her suitcase, took out the Bible, and opened it to a place she had marked.

"Let's keep it short," said the man.

"Listen," said Joan. "'For I am come to set a man at variance against his father, and the daughter against her mother . . . And a man's foes shall be they of his own household.'"

"That's in the Bible?"

Joan held the book open for him to see.

"I can't read without my glasses," he said. "But you can't go by that. It was a different time. The early church, they were under a lot of pressure."

"I suppose you're right," said Joan. "I don't believe it's the word of God anyway. At one time I did, but now I'm not sure."

"A pack of tall tales, handed down, over generations."

"And if that's the case," said Joan, "then you no more have

the right to say 'I do this because of the Bible' than you would to say 'I do this because of —'"

"The *Sporting News*."

"I came to this city on business," said Joan.

"I know."

"How?"

"The way you're dressed."

"Oh, right. But I also — and I see this now, and I saw it before — I was also looking for something to force the issue. To be hypnotized, or fall in love, or be taken hostage in a failed heist, and everything would change. Instead I have to do it myself."

"Uh-huh."

"What about you?"

"What do you want?"

"Well, it's just that you've been down, and — I don't know if this is presumptuous —"

"Absolutely, I've been down," he said. "They once called me a natural at deciphering industrial codes, but I could never forget what the lawyer told me. 'Succinct answers make succinct depositions.' Imagine hearing those words, what they would do to a young mind. I wish I could forget them. And they told me I could not join the war effort until I was ready to dress for success. And they said I knew Somoza, but that was another lie. And ever since then I haven't felt right. What time do you have?"

Joan pulled back the sleeve of her jacket. "Quarter of ten."

"I've got to run."

They stood. The man rolled and tied his sleeping bag with swift, forceful motions, as if roping a small animal.

Joan walked around until she found a bus depot. Inside, a demonstration of Irish dance was going on, and this made it hard for her to concentrate. She was tired and hungry. The dancers linked arms, stomping the tiles. Joan walked along the ticket counters, looking for the shortest line, the clerk with the kindest eyes. She chose a young woman in a turtleneck sweater.

"I don't care where I go. I just want to get out of town for a few days."

"How about Lonachan?" said the clerk. "A lot of people go up there to see what the tornado did. Plus it's got the effigy mounds and the reform school."

"When was the tornado?"

"Two summers ago," the clerk said. "But it's still damaged."

"One, please."

Joan boarded the bus. The engine was running, and it was very hot inside. She sank gratefully into a seat. How many nights had it been since she had slept well? She could not count them, or remember where she had been, or when. Her seat-mate was a traveling salesman reading a science-fiction novel called *The Woman with Many Arms.* He saw her looking at the book and asked the purpose of her trip. Her mouth moved, but she said nothing. He waited. She remembered a church pageant in her youth when she had drawn laughter by nervously repeating the title of the piece she was supposed to say — *A Gift at Our House, A Gift at Our House* — while outside the church the wind gusted and icicles cracked against the windows. Where was that? Indiana . . . The woman on the cover of the book had four arms, reaching out like the arms of Shiva.

Dr. Palomino took two sack lunches to the Stone City art museum at noon. He was a benefactor of the museum, but he always had a hard time finding his way in. It seemed that you entered through the freight elevator. *Oh, this modern architecture, where is it headed?* he thought.

Once inside, he looked at the exhibit book but barely registered its contents, because he was thinking about Joan. He believed — in fact, he had read — that promiscuity results from a lack of identity; thus you are always looking for new bodies through which to discover your true self (not having found it in other bodies, grown familiar). And he thought it was true that he was most troubled by lust when he felt it least likely that he would make a mark in his field. However, he was also troubled by lust when things appeared to be going his way. At those times his desire seemed less like trouble than like a generous impulse to share his happening self with the uninitiated. Where was she?

He was standing in a room full of landscape paintings. The artist had a facility for clouds. He had rendered them in shades of blue, violet, and green. They lorded it over the life forms in the paintings — a sharecropper, a mule, a farmer and his little son.

Dr. Palomino thought he had pinpointed the very moment when he had begun to lose the sense of himself that was reportedly the key to a balanced libido. It was at his wedding, many years ago. It was a hot day; later there would be thunderstorms. The ceremony was not long, but given the darkening sky, everyone was anxious to get out of the church. Nonetheless, when it came time to kiss the bride, the doctor did not hurry. A moment of thought seemed worthwhile. He had witnessed other weddings where the bride and groom, in their eagerness to get through the ceremony without making any mistakes, would bump their lips together in a pro forma sort of way, and he wanted to avoid this. And as he studied his bride — her upturned face, her frightened eyes, the interesting thing that her sisters had done with her hair — he heard his own father, speaking in a stage whisper from the front row: "Kiss her, kiss her, for God's sake."

Well, maybe he didn't say "For God's sake." But he definitely told Dr. Palomino to hurry and kiss the bride, which he did, but even as he did, the seed of doubt was planted. Was he Stephen Palomino, M.D., with ten years of the finest training behind him, the family practitioner in command of all aspects of his life, or was he someone who could not stumble his way through even this most memorized of social rituals without the pathetic coaching of his father?

He *had* known what he was doing, that was the hell of it. He had been trying to work a variation on the norm, but he knew what the norm was and did not need his father to draw a diagram and wave it before the congregation.

Could this be where his restlessness began?

He looked at his watch. Then he moved on to the next room, which featured paintings of country fairs. A clown in white makeup and a millstone collar held a small monkey before a backdrop of sagging canvas; three women posed half dressed on a stage, their backs to the painter; a woman in a burlap bathing suit stood blankly, with an emerald snake coiled three times around her body. The spectators in the paintings were an odd lot — rural folks with sunken cheeks, leering businessmen, and agitated old women. Only the clown with the monkey had drawn a wholesome audience, but there were not many in it.

The doctor hurried away from the carnival pictures; they seemed to indict him. The next room had so many paintings of hallways, doors, and stairs that you wouldn't know which way to turn if you had to get out. Several of the hallways featured a crooked portrait of an old man with a long beard and restless eyes. In others, a chalky ghost hovered a foot or so above the floor. These paintings filled the doctor with anxiety.

He went out into the courtyard of the museum and sat on a bench to eat lunch. Joan's absence might represent a disavowal of their night together. He blinked rapidly, remembering the way she had looked in the light that filtered through the hotel window. *Kiss her, you fool, kiss the woman.* He felt no rejection and only a little disappointment. But he knew he would keep his distance from here on out. When he saw her, he would make some innocuous remark, nothing that would hurt her, just some commonplace.

He got up to leave. Maybe he'd go shopping. A new pair of shoes always put him in a better frame of mind.

The bus arrived in Lonachan late in the afternoon. The town had a tragic atmosphere, and Joan realized while walking to the police station that the trees had all been sheared off at a height of ten or twelve feet.

"They're here," said the sergeant at the front desk, as if he knew her. "Arrived today. The calendars, I mean. We are the ones. The men of the police department. Well, I shouldn't say men, because there are two women as well. The year 2000 — think of it, where has the time gone?"

He showed her a calendar, turned to a color photograph of himself working, shirtless, on the engine of a pickup. "Not bad for someone who never modeled," he said.

"You're Mr. February," said Joan.

"I know, a nothing month. I asked for September. What do you need?"

Joan had given this some thought. Her best option seemed to be the appearance of having a destination. She knew three things about the town. A tornado from the past could not be a destination. The effigy mounds could be, but they might not be much to look at. That left the reform school. She might even find a job there.

"I'm looking for the reform school," she said.

"Follow me in your car," said another officer, dusting the floor of the station with a mop.

Joan explained that she had come on the bus.

"I'll take you," he said. "My shift is over, I'm going up there anyway, and I'm tired of hearing about that grotesque calendar."

He and Joan got into his cruiser and rode through the broad streets of the town. Joan asked where he'd been during the tornado.

"In my basement, under a pallet," he said. "Where we're going got it pretty bad, though. Now, you're aware the school is closed."

"Oh," Joan said.

"Six or seven months ago," said the policeman. "They still have community activities in the gym. Were you one of the graduates?"

Joan shook her head.

"Because every once in a while we still get alumni, come back to see the school. You'd be surprised how successful some of them are. The reason I'm going there is we're rehearsing a play. *The Seagull,* by Anton Chekhov."

Joan sat up straight and turned to him. Her voice surprised her with its hoarseness. "I know that play. Mister, I've been in that play. I was Masha."

"No lie," said the policeman. "Because guess who I am: Semyon Semyonovich."

"My hopeless lover . . ."

"'What terrible weather! Two whole days of it!'"

"'There are waves on the lake,'" said Joan. "'Tremendous ones.'"

He laughed and turned the wheel. "Tell me something, because I'm curious. When you were Masha, did you take snuff?"

Joan gave him a look of professional reproach, going back through years, an actress again. "You have no choice if you're going to be Masha. But you can pretend."

"I wish everyone thought like you. We've got snuff, but our Masha won't go near it."

They went into the school, down a dark corridor, and through the doors of the gym. The actors were on the stage, performing a scene. Wooden tables were all around. Joan stood below the footlights as the policeman climbed the stairs. The woman who would not take snuff was asking the writer Trigorin to sign books for her.

And Joan whispered the line with her: "Just put 'To Masha, who doesn't know where she comes from or what she's doing on this earth.'"

14 · Lyris

CHARLES CALLED Lyris and Micah into the living room on Monday morning before school. He sat listening to the news on the radio, pulling on socks and boots. His socks did not match, but he didn't seem to mind or even necessarily notice.

A man on the radio said that it was going to be a windy week and now was the time to put away any summer furniture still out in the yard. A woman on the radio said now was the time to buy a hog if you had the freezer for it. The man said he had been unable to get the song "Winter Wonderland" out of his head for two years running, so he was ready for the change of season. The woman said they shouldn't joke about such a thing, because nuisance music might be a serious problem for some people. The man said he was not joking, he was one of those for whom it was a serious problem.

Charles shut the radio off. "Did you feed the goat?"

They said they had not.

"Here's how it's going to work. Lyris will feed the goat in the morning and Micah will feed the goat at night."

Lyris turned to go feed the goat.

"Wait a minute," said Charles.

"Are you and Mom getting divorced?" said Micah. He held a plate with toast on it.

"What did I say last night?" said Charles.

"That she will be home today."

"Is that what I said?"

"That you weren't sure when she'd be home," said Lyris.

Micah folded to the floor, cross-legged and crying. He put the plate on the rug. "I want her here."

"When her work is done," said Charles. "It might be a while. We thought it was going to be for the weekend, but now we don't know. They chose her. Of course she would rather be with you. She didn't ask for it."

"Is that what she said?" said Micah.

"She said she'll be home in the spring," said Charles. "What does crying get you?"

Micah spoke with a trembling voice: "Nothing."

He and Lyris rode to school on a snub-nosed yellow bus that pitched and shuddered in the wind. The treelines were bright and slanted beyond the fields. Lyris sat far from Micah, as was dictated by the difference in their ages. She knew more than he did. The work Joan had gone to the city for did not figure into Joan's absence. Lyris was tempted to think *Left once, left again,* but she knew that would only be paranoia and that in the world Joan had decided not to come back to, she played a fairly minor role. In this light, the blood ties that the Home Bringers put all their emphasis on seemed insubstantial and even arbitrary. Anyone could be anyone's child.

When she was younger, Lyris had sometimes wondered how it would be if she were someone else. She did not imagine being a person in better circumstances, because she had always had heat, a roof, a bed, and food. Instead she imagined being a child in a war-torn province, what that would be like. She had sometimes come perilously close to wondering herself out of existence. But she rarely thought that way anymore.

Lyris had art history just before lunch. The class was an odd mix of people who cared quite a lot about the topic and people who didn't care about it at all. This had to do with the way the class had been filled. Art history was mandatory for all the seniors who would be going on the spring trip to Paris, but a fair number of these students had chosen Paris (over Amarillo, the alternate destination) not because of its cultural treasures but because getting there would require a flight across the ocean. Some of them had never flown before, and they reasoned that if they were going to do it, they might as well go as far as possible.

In any case, the students who did not care about art history sometimes tried to disrupt the classroom experience of those who took it seriously. One of the forms this disruption took was the throwing of the methamphetamine tablets called white cross. The idea was to lob the pills in such a way that the person you were trying to bother would have to either retrieve and hide them or risk being caught with illegal drugs in the vicinity of his or her desk. Explanation was out of the question. It would amount to ratting, and no one could rat. In other words, planting white cross on someone was regarded as less of a sin than disclosing who had planted it on you. Lyris did not make up the rules. She sat neither in the front nor in the back. She thought of the long narrow room as a river and her desk near the window as a sandbar on which she might avoid the currents.

The teacher was a handsome if careworn man who had been a painter himself. He had suffered disappointments, among which teaching in this school seemed to be one, and he tended to portray the history of art as an unbroken chain of disastrous events. Today's topic was a French artist who came to prominence after painting a portrait of the empress Josephine cupping a plum in one hand and a yellow pullet in the other. For a while the young painter held Napoleon's favor — the emperor presented him with a walking stick with a silver handle. When Napoleon divorced Josephine, though, the artist fell from grace and joined the French army. Wounded at Borodino, he starved to death on the retreat from Moscow and was found with Napoleon's walking stick clutched in his icy hands. A tragedy, for salt cod was on the way.

"How many of us would show that kind of dedication?" asked the teacher. "Or are we too comfortable, with our soft pillows and our prepared foods? I think perhaps we are. And yet that is what it takes — to be willing to insulate the walls of your house with your rejected paintings and never experience a moment's doubt."

This was not the first time the teacher had mentioned the use of unsold paintings as insulation. Another thing he sometimes brought up was how he was saving big boxes in case his radical views got him fired and evicted.

One of the students now asked in what way the story of the painter-turned-soldier demonstrated dedication to art. He stood to ask his question. "I mean, he died in a war — got that. But what's it got to do with painting?"

The teacher turned to face the blackboard. A white pill bounced off the boy's lumberjack shirt. The teacher wrote *war* and *painting* on the board. "Anyone?"

A good long silence followed. "Because painting is like a war," said Lyris. She was only guessing. Painting did not seem at all like a war to her. This was just her go-along-to-get-along nature in operation.

The teacher beamed. It was not because she had found the answer he intended her to find. In fact, the boy had raised a good point. So far as the teacher knew, the painter had never picked up a brush after the imperial divorce. The lecture had arrived at a logical impasse, due to the teacher's desire to leave the students with the image of a dead artist on the side of the road. So he was glad to have any answer. He drew an equal sign between the two words, stepped back to consider the equation, and then underlined the words *war* and *painting*.

Meanwhile, some of the students pantomimed the eating of porridge, as was their practice when Lyris spoke up in class. They did so with various hand-to-mouth motions that would have confused anyone who did not know they were trying to make fun of a person who had once lived in an orphanage.

Lyris smiled shyly — she could take a joke with the best of them. Was she so pathetic, she asked herself, that she welcomed even ridicule? She hoped not, but kept on smiling.

Juniors and seniors were allowed to leave the school grounds at lunchtime. Lyris, Mercedes Wonsmos, Echo Anderson, and Octavia or Taffy Perry walked up to the Lake Park Tavern along with another young woman, the senior Jade Teensma. Jade bought all her clothes in the Twin Cities, or "the Cities," as she called them, and had gained early admission to the University of Minnesota, and was going to Paris in the spring. Her future seemed suspended above them, shining like the sun. Today she wore platform sandals and a long silver coat.

Lyris looked forward to ordering hash browns at the Lake Park. She walked a little ahead of the other girls, going along the alley, thinking of the painter whose career was ruined by Napoleon's divorce.

"So what happened Saturday night?" said Mercedes. "Did you pull a Dun and Bradstreet?"

Echo tugged on the sleeve of Lyris's jacket. "Mercy has a question."

Lyris turned and walked backward with her hands in her pockets. "I'm sorry?"

"With Billy Follard," said Mercedes. "You know what I'm talking about. You're within range of my voice. Did you do anything you shouldn't have?"

"It didn't go very well," said Lyris.

"It was ever thus," said Jade.

"Boys on one side, girls on the other," said Echo.

"Nothing happened," said Lyris.

Mercedes took Lyris's hands in her own. "Tell the truth. Because this is important." The girls stood looking at Lyris with light in their eyes. They seemed to want a certain answer from her.

"Nothing did," said Lyris. "We went to a grain elevator. We went to a bridge. He told me a story about Baby Mahoney."

"The wild child?" said Mercedes.

"Not that old saw," said Jade.

"Then he wouldn't take me home, so I found my own way."

"I don't buy that for a second," said Mercedes.

"I do," said Octavia.

"Swear it on your mother's grave," Echo suggested.

"My mother's alive."

"But eventually."

"She doesn't have to swear," said Octavia. "I believe her. Every situation doesn't end in sex."

Jade brought out a pack of herbal cigarettes, lit one by cupping it against the wind, and handed the pack and lighter around. "Let's hurry up," she said, and they did, each thinking her own private thoughts and considering what Octavia had said.

Follard worked in a shoestore in Stone City. It did not seem a fitting occupation for a badass, and he felt this himself, but it couldn't be helped. He had been hired by his uncle, who owned the store. In the twenties, a famous bank robber had

bought a pair of blucher oxfords here before being apprehended in another county. Somehow the shoes had been returned to the store, and they still resided in a glass case behind
the counter. They had more or less collapsed over the years,
and the toe caps looked stiff and set. Sometimes old men
brought their grandchildren in to see the gangster's shoes, as if
to say, "Let them be a lesson." Once, after Follard had begun
working at the store, he dreamed that his uncle was chasing
him between the racks, wearing the shoes on his hands. When
he woke up, he had to walk around the house to make sure no
one was there.

Follard was suffering. When he reached for the top shelves,
he felt a sharpness in his heart. Naturally, all the shoes people
wanted that day were up high. The store was busy for a Monday. When he answered the phone, the caller would ask if
he had been running. He refused to admit to himself that
his ribs might have been broken by Tiny Darling. At noon he
walked down the street to a diner, where a man having the
hot beef launched into a sneering tirade against the president.
The monologue seemed aimed at Follard, who only looked
around. He didn't care about the president, so this was no way
to start something with him, nor was he in any condition to re-
spond. He bought an egg salad sandwich and a newspaper
and walked back to the store, where he meant to eat his lunch
at a card table in the supply room. When he reached for the
glass door, the pain brought him low, so that he was kneeling
there, with newspaper and sandwich spilled on the sidewalk,
when his uncle came to the front of the store.

"Get up," he said.

"I think my ribs are broken."

"You've been acting funny all day," said his uncle. He
helped Follard to his feet and brought him inside, then dialed
the hands of a cardboard clock to two o'clock and hung it on

the door. He directed Follard to sit in one of the trying-on chairs and brought him a paper cup of water. With an ease indicating long years of practice, he hooked a low padded bench with his foot, slid it over, and sat down.

"What happened?"

Follard drank the water and sprawled in the chair. "I fell last night," he said. "I fell against the stair thing. The post."

"Your aunt said a plumber came to see you. Did this happen before or after the plumber came?"

"I don't know."

"Did you fight the plumber?"

Follard crushed the paper cup in his hand. "I fought the plumber."

"Were you at fault?"

"I am hurting! Do you hear me?"

"Yes, I hear you."

Just then Dr. Palomino opened the door and leaned into the shop. "Closed, are you?"

Follard's uncle stood up. "Is it something quick? If it's a small item, such as a shoelace or mink oil, I could ring you up."

"I'm looking for a pair of shoes. I don't like to rush into these things."

"It's my nephew — claims his ribs are broken." He waved his hand, a gesture that meant *Oh, these kids and their ribs.*

"Want me to take a look? I am a doctor."

"How lucky. Come on in. We'll give you cost plus ten. He was in a fight."

"That's what it usually is with ribs," said Dr. Palomino. "Fights and car wrecks and team sports. Get his shirt off. Let's hope it isn't flail chest. I don't suppose you know what a flail is, but your uncle might. A flail is an ancient threshing tool with a free-swinging wooden stick."

Follard relayed his symptoms while his uncle pulled the sleeves of his shirt. The doctor listened, stealing glances at the new line of hard-soled moccasins.

Octavia Perry gave Lyris a ride home from school. Along the road they stopped to watch someone combining. Five spears of gleaming silver combed through cornstalks, which vibrated in their grip. In the combine's wake, the ground was shorn and brushy. Lauryn Hill sang on the radio about "that thing, that thing, that thing," but then the combine drowned her out, harvesting the rows nearest the road.

Octavia took a manila envelope from above the visor. "I want you to give this to Jerry," she said. "I know that nothing really stops you from opening and reading it, but I don't think that you will."

"What's it all about?"

"He'll get it," said Octavia.

Lyris put the envelope in her backpack. "Will do."

Octavia curled her hair behind her ears. "If you have to know, my parents found out about the setup."

"Jerry Tate?" said Lyris. "My uncle."

"I call him Mr. Postman," said Octavia.

"You have a setup with Jerry Tate?"

"It began at a chess exhibit at the state fair. It turned out both of us loved the game. My mother is livid. She says, 'I'll state-fair *you*.'"

Octavia looked out the window. The red combine had stopped beside a green wagon. She seemed peaceful with her decision, whatever it might be.

"That is a bangin' combine," she said.

The farmer opened the cab door and climbed down the metal stairs. He was a young man, but his hair was shaggy and streaked with gray.

"I know him," said Octavia. "It's Albert Robeshaw." She

and Lyris got out of the car and crossed the ditch, batting weeds from their way. The farmer removed cinched leather gloves and held them bunched in one hand as he leaned an elbow on a metal-capped post of the fence.

"I used to baby-sit you," he said.

"And you weren't ever going to farm," said Octavia. "That's what you told me. You were going to travel all over the world and never be a farmer."

"I did travel some. Made it to Thailand."

"Albert, this is Lyris."

Albert and Lyris shook hands. He smiled and looked into her eyes until she blinked. His eyes were brown and kindly mocking. He slapped his gloves against his palm. "I'm going to run this out and then you can go along with me a round or two if you want."

Albert went back up the steps and cranked the combine so corn began pouring from the hooded spout in a uniform yellow spiral that hissed and clattered into the wagon. Dust rose, swirling and thinning in the blue air.

When the wagon was full, Albert, Octavia, and Lyris climbed into the cab of the combine, and Albert eased it into gear. He seemed glad to have company. "The corn's standing good this year," he said, loud enough to be heard over the engine and the augers. "Some years it gets broke over. But this way you can run the snoots high and it makes it easier going."

"Snoots?" said Lyris.

"These big silver things that you see up front, pulling in the corn," said Albert. "Some years you have to run them so low they catch in the dirt. It can mess you up pretty good."

Albert aimed the blades between the cornrows, where they yanked the stalks violently down. The ears of corn boiled up to the hopper.

"Did you like Thailand?" said Octavia.

"It was good. The Buddhists there I hadn't known much

about. This idea of lighting your own lamp. I saw the Temple of the Emerald Buddha. There's a place of great peace. When I ran out of money, I came home."

Lyris looked out across the country, which sloped to a distant valley and climbed again to the horizon. The geography of farming was inescapable, the striped pattern of crops harvested and crops standing, the patchwork of fields and pastures and water. Power pylons ran down the trough of the valley, and vehicles flashed on distant highways.

"Is all this corn the same?" she said.

"No," said Albert. "Some does better in wet, some in dry. Some matures in a hundred days, some in a hundred and eight. The long-maturing ones yield better, but not if you get an early frost. What you're doing by planting four, five varieties, see, is limiting your risk."

"You sound like a farmer to me," said Octavia, pressed against the glass in the corner of the cab. Plowbirds with V-shaped wings darted and dove, following the combine.

"This is the best time of year, really," said Albert. "All the stuff we've done so far isn't worth anything until you pick it. With planting and spraying, you know you're doing it, but it don't look much different anyway. But this here, as you go across, it's gone, so you can watch yourself going."

Later a pheasant flew up in front of the combine with a hard clipped beating of wings and coasted low into a thicket. Albert said that some farmers let hunters stand at the end of the rows, waiting for the pheasants to come their way, but he did not care for anyone shooting while he was riding high in a glass box.

Even given this instructive detour, Lyris got home before Micah, owing to the one-thirty release of upperclassmen. She put her backpack in her room and then went down to clean the kitchen. She began by putting the curtains back up. Their rings hung on dowels with nothing to keep them from falling, but for now they looked like regular curtains in a regular house. She scrubbed the stove with steel wool. She even cleaned the vise grips for the burner with the missing knob. On the table she found the penknife that she would have sworn she had returned to Follard. She threw it in the trash. Shoes and boots, pairs and strays, she lined up by the stairs.

From the kitchen she moved into the back yard, where she folded the lawn chairs and carried them to the barn. Then she walked out along the railroad tracks, picking wild asparagus for supper. The goat was in a ditch, trying to make itself inconspicuous. Asparagus in one hand and the goat's collar in the other, she headed back to the house. Railroad spikes in the grass reminded her of something that had happened while she was living with her foster parents Pete and Jackie. Mail arrived one day with Lyris's name on it. The tract inside was titled *How to Derail Any Train with Items Found in the Average Home Workshop*. Reading this document, Lyris learned of many shockingly simple methods by which a train could be derailed, including one described in the Warren Report on the assassination of President John F. Kennedy.

When Lyris showed the pamphlet to Pete and Jackie, Pete said it was meant for him and must have come to her by mistake. Lyris asked why he would want to derail a train, and he said he didn't but some friends of his were interested in the topic. Lyris then asked why Pete's friends would want to derail a train, and he said he didn't think they did either — their interest was of a more scholarly nature — but if they did, it would be because industrial society was unjust. People could get killed, said Lyris. Pete said that no one was considering derailing a passenger train, and Jackie at this point chimed in to say that Lyris was thinking in the way that society wanted her to think.

Pete agreed. "Look at you," he said. "You have nothing,

you have less than nothing, and yet your first thought is to protect the freight of some uncaring rail monopoly."

Such thinking was not Lyris's fault, Jackie said. It was something everyone had to work past. Lyris nodded, but her mind would not yield the point. She thought that Pete and Jackie were the ones who had it wrong.

15 · Charles

CHARLES'S LAST JOB that day involved water dripping from the ceiling of the music room in the elementary school. Mrs. Harad, the principal, had once bought a field spaniel in a deal brokered by Charles, and this was one reason Charles got the call. Another was that Mrs. Harad wanted to reward the family for Joan's support during the evolution scandal. So it was that the principal escorted the plumber into the music room, where they stood looking at the cracked old plaster as if at the vault of heaven. Charles said they were going to have to pop that ceiling open. He had found that customers liked it when he spoke this way. The room was full of students singing in their light high voices as drops of water fell into a bronze kettle. Micah smiled while hiding his face behind a songbook turned to "The Streets of Laredo."

"Get six jolly cowboys to carry my coffin," sang the children. "Get six pretty maidens to bear up my pall."

Charles steadied a high wooden ladder and climbed. With a Kafer saw he scored the wet plaster so that it broke and fell, with wet heavy sounds, down to the blue tiles. Mrs. Harad snapped her fingers, and the music teacher waved the children from their seats, through the doorway, and into the hall. They kept singing all the while. The music teacher revised the lyrics with directions on where they were going: "We beat the drum slowly and played the fife lowly, and bitterly wept as we moved single-file to the cafeteria."

"What a wreck of a school," said Mrs. Harad.

Plaster kept falling. When the hole was big enough, Charles put his hand up inside the ceiling. "It's a cold supply line," he said. The rest of the afternoon was given over to the repair. Charles shut off the water and drained the pipes by running the faucets above and below until they were dry. An elbow fitting was leaking. Charles melted the solder with a propane torch and pulled the fitting off with big-jawed pliers. He cleaned the ends of the pipes and scoured the new piece he meant to put on. From time to time the principal came by to monitor the work, and on one of these visits she asked how Joan was.

Charles looked down from the ladder. "She's gone off and won't be home till spring."

"That's too long."

Charles brushed flux onto the copper and fitted the pipe ends into the new joint. "Well, I wasn't expecting it, though maybe I should have been. And Micah's got a cold and Lyris is being pursued by trash."

"What a fellow ought to do is get drunk," said Mrs. Harad. Then she told a story about her honeymoon. In a bend in the road, she and her husband lost control of the little Triumph motorcycle on which they had departed from the church.

"They all said, 'Ride it,'" she said. "You know how it is when people at a wedding get an idea that the bride and groom must do some particular thing. 'Ride that bike.' We went down on some loose gravel we didn't see until we were in it."

"And what's the point?"

"Just that things never seem to go right."

Charles had not really blamed himself for Joan's decision. All that drove her lay inside her, he thought. He would have a hard time leaving the house, leaving Micah and Lyris. But this might be laziness, not honor. Life mattered more to Joan than it did to him. She thought there was a meaning she must track down. Maybe he should have bought her that tourmaline solitaire he had seen in Stone City. Maybe he should have married her on Main Street and not in the back room of a drugstore. Long ago he had stopped believing that his acts could move her, but he could be wrong.

He picked up Micah after school and together they went to the gun shop. On the way, the boy told Charles about the "self-esteem car wash" his class had had that day. No cars were involved, only children pretending to be cars. Each kid walked a gauntlet of classmates, who had been directed to call out whatever they considered to be the student's strong points.

"What'd they say about you?" said Charles.

"That I'm a good reader," said Micah. "And I don't abuse drugs."

"Well, they're right," said Charles. "You know, it reminds me of the sticks, which we had when I was a kid."

"What's that?"

"There were six or seven of us who walked home from school together. We'd go down the alley between the restaurant and the bank, past a big pile of sticks. I don't remember how it started, but it became a tradition almost that everyone would pick up sticks and throw them at one of us, who had been picked beforehand to be the victim."

"Did the person know?"

"Usually not," said Charles, "because it wouldn't happen every day. And lots of times you would have been told that someone else was going to be the one. But sometimes you did know. You could just tell."

"Daddy, that's pathetic."

They had come to a high gravel crossroads, and Charles could see that no one was coming. He hit the gas. The van jumped the crown of the road and crashed down on the other side.

"It wasn't that bad," said Charles. "Even when all your friends were throwing sticks at you. Getting hit by sticks is not as painful as it sounds. And the minute you picked up a stick and turned to throw it back, they all ran. We weren't that serious about hurting each other."

Charles and Micah got out at the gun shop, and Charles took his stepfather's shotgun from the back of the van. The brother and sister who owned the shop were sitting in director's chairs, watching the Weather Channel. Clear and cold was the forecast. Charles wondered how much of their day must be spent doing nothing. It wouldn't be easy.

"Here's that gun I was telling you about," said Charles. "The one that a few days ago I thought I would never get."

"Good for you," said the brother. He took the shotgun and looked it over. "I've never seen anything quite like it."

"We're not buying just now," said the sister.

"I thought you'd be interested," said Charles. "Not to buy it, just, you know, professional curiosity. And I need a couple boxes of four-ten shells."

"We've got a special on Winchester seven and a half," said the brother.

"I'll bet I know someone who would like a gun safety coloring book," said the sister.

Charles purchased three boxes of shells, and they all went outside to try the gun. There was a mowed field behind the shop. The brother had a trap mounted on the back of a pickup so that he could sit on the tailgate and fire the clay targets. He took one from a cardboard box in the bed and cocked the trap as Charles stood and loaded the gun. Charles missed, and missed again. He cracked open the barrels and pulled out two spent shells the color of tomatoes. The smell of the burned powder came up. There was a time when the misses would have bothered him, but not today. The terra-cotta disk of the third clay spun flat over the field. He swung through it, pulled the trigger, and followed up clean. The target broke apart, pieces tumbling into the grass.

"Sporting clays," said the sister.

They took turns with the gun. The sister was a better shot than Charles, and the brother was best. The siblings called "Pull" in bland voices. Very likely they went to events. But even the brother missed sometimes.

"Nothing wrong with that," he said, handing the shotgun to Charles.

"Sweet little gun," said the sister. "I like it with a four-ten, because it's not easy."

"I know," said the brother. "I had forgotten."

"Let me try," said Micah, who had been sitting in the open door of the truck, looking at the coloring book and the shooting. He took his turn, with Charles's arms steadying his own.

When twilight was coming on, Charles walked back to the van with Micah and the shotgun.

"Do you think Joan will be home yet?" said Micah.

Charles shook his head. "I told you, buddy. It's going to be a while."

"Cross your fingers."

So Charles drove home with crossed fingers riding the rim of the steering wheel. Micah turned in his seat and put his feet up on the edge of the door.

"My feet are closer than they appear," he said.

Jerry came over for supper that night. He chopped carrots with a serrated blade while Lyris opened the creaking oven door from time to time to look at a casserole. Micah sat at the kitchen desk coloring a picture of a game warden by the light of the green glass banker's lamp. Charles set the table with chipped white plates. He and Jerry had drinks and talked about the truck-mounted trap, and why more things weren't truck-mounted, and how whoever came up with such an idea was probably raking in the scratch. Then they all sat down to eat.

The casserole was made of eggplant and asparagus. It needed seasonings they did not have, but everyone ate a fair share. Charles bent to the table, a forearm laid on the edge. He drank water from one glass and whiskey from another. Lyris would put a forkful of food in her mouth and chew mindfully, gazing around the kitchen as if seeing it for the first time. Micah had arranged dark red shotgun shells around his plate. Jerry knifed a slab of butter onto a crust of bread. No one talked about Joan. It seemed unfair to her that in her absence everything was so normal. Of course, things could still go very wrong; it was only seven o'clock.

After the dishes were done, Charles took his whiskey out to the porch, where he sat with the goat and looked out at the railroad tracks and the woods beyond. The goat seemed to have adapted to the porch, and vice versa, since all the things that she might have become tangled in had been removed by Charles, Lyris, or Micah, or by the goat herself. Charles drank the whiskey slowly but steadily, and he realized that he might well be getting drunk, as Mrs. Harad had advised. But he got drunk so rarely now; it was nothing like the old days of kicking down doors, of threats made and carried through or foolishly messed up. This was more of a composed drunkenness, a receptivity, and he thought he could almost feel the pulse of the night, as if his heart were beating to its time.

Micah came out when his homework was finished, and Charles sent him back inside to get a coat on. Together they watched the train come through at a quarter of nine. It was all grain hoppers and boxcars, some open, some closed, clattering and rocking, along tracks known to be rough. Micah wanted to hear the old story of how Charles had hopped a freight out west, only to have it go about a mile before stopping on a siding in the middle of nowhere for the night. Charles had ended up sleeping like a troll under a wooden bridge, or so he told it, playing up the parts that made him seem ridiculous. Micah loved every word.

In the kitchen, Lyris gave Jerry the message from Octavia, and he read her lush handwriting under the banker's lamp:

> Meet me at the E. at midnight.
>
>> Sincerely,
>> Octavia

Heading home in the car, Jerry felt both charmed and excited by the message. The "E." stood for the Elephant, as anyone from around here could guess. The abbreviation seemed like just the sort of endearing feint at intrigue a young mind would concoct. An older person would have written the location out in block letters, breathing with difficulty. And the "Sincerely" was a totally disarming usage.

He stopped at the all-night car wash, a lonely chain of dark bays lit by high, stark electric globes. There was no attendant; whatever washing was going to take place had to be done by the customer. Jerry pulled smashed bills from his pants pockets, smoothed them flat on the hood of the car, and fed them into the change machine. He mopped the car with a drizzle of soapy gray water from a long-handled brush. The rinse cycle was relatively violent. The high-powered nozzle bucked against his hands as if it would fly away. He drove out of the bay and parked by the vacuum cleaner. Whatever happened, his car would be immaculate. He dropped beer cans and cigarette cellophanes and undelivered mail into a trash barrel. With a sodden cloth from a vending machine, he polished the dashboard and door panels until they gleamed as if a quart of salad oil had detonated in the front seat. He even cleaned out the glove compartment. His map of the Midwest was outdated, faded, splitting along the folds. It depicted long-finished highways as broken blue lines that suggested a bright future for driving.

He got back on the road. All this activity, he knew, was partly a means of avoiding the question of what he should do when he met Octavia.

Before he could decide, his car was overtaken by a police cruiser. Although flashing no lights and sounding no siren, it pulled abreast in the passing lane and stayed even with him. Through the windows, Jerry could see Earl the deputy waving sternly at the shoulder. Jerry pulled over, and the cruiser blocked his way. Then the lights came on, turning slowly, red, blue, and yellow. It seemed there were more colors every year. Both men got out of their cars.

"Nice night," said Jerry.

Earl walked back, shining a flashlight on the ground. "Say, you still got that keg?"

"Maybe. Why?"

"The liquor store's looking for it."

"I just came from the car wash."

"Well, that's great."

"Why don't I take it back when I'm done with it?"

"Look, Jerry, I'm not going to fuck around on this," said Earl. "All I been hearing about all day's that jackass keg. Turns out the kid come in there this morning or, I don't know, over the weekend, saying he wants his deposit back, since it was stolen through no fault of his own."

"That's debatable."

"They don't want the deposit anyway. The whole theory of the deposit is to make sure the kegs come back. Which I would think is a fairly obvious point. What do you mean, when you're done with it? Isn't it getting kind of flat?"

"Come on over and pick it up," Jerry said. "You don't have to get all martial law about it."

"It's a hassle, and that's all it is," said Earl. "But I owe the liquor store guys a favor, since they fund some of our activities."

Earl floored it, but Jerry's car could not keep up with the cruiser's V-8 or V-10 or whatever V it was. Jerry dropped back, but he tried to keep the taillights in sight, because he half suspected a trick was being played on him. There was no need to hurry. There were hours to go before midnight.

With their separate preoccupations — Earl's thinking of the runaway keg and Jerry's striving to keep the cruiser lights in range — both drivers passed a gas station at the intersection of 56 and the Chesley Road without seeing Follard, who stood at the lone pump beside the ice machine, holding his side with one hand while running kerosene into a blue plastic container. Anyone who knew about Follard's history might have wondered what he had in mind. The counterman, however, knew no one in the county very well. He had come all the way from Tuscaloosa to deliver a diesel Mercedes and decided to stay awhile. All he said, after holding Follard's twenty to the light and then giving him his change, was "Y'all have a nice night." In fairness, anyone, no matter his origin or what he knew of local lore, would have been hard-pressed to deprive Follard of his commercial right to buy the same five gallons of kero anyone else could buy.

Follard's condition fell short of flail chest. Dr. Palomino had said so, and the emergency room doctors had agreed. They had taken X-rays and prescribed Tylenol with codeine. They gave him instructions on allowing the ribs to fix themselves.

They advised rest and deep breathing. But Follard could not rest. He had decided that Charles Darling must be hurt in order to save Lyris's reputation.

His thinking ran like this: If Lyris had been dishonored, then Charles might have been justified in beating him up. But she had not been dishonored. She was all right. He had seen that she got out of the river, had called to her, had tried to say that all was forgotten. She fell; it was nothing he had intended. This very morning he had watched as she got off the bus, walking ably, unbroken. He could see her; she couldn't see him, but she was all right. Therefore — and this was a leap Follard easily made — if he did not pay Charles back, it would amount to confirmation of the notion that Lyris had been dishonored.

He had formulated this logic late in the afternoon, while resting and breathing deeply on his mattress in the house.

Now he lifted the kerosene into his car. This hurt. Five gallons weigh a lot to someone in pain. He set the tank upright between the front and back seats and drove to a roadhouse. He sat at a picnic table indoors, eating northern pike and home fries. The guilty smell of kerosene was on his hands. He knew that if he were a stronger man, he could skip the whole thing. This was something his uncle had once said, about another act of revenge Follard had had under consideration. But he was not strong, and he was not brave. Neither was he trustworthy or loyal. He envied his aunt and uncle, the way they moved blindly forward — honest, hardworking, laughable, as if someone were going to reward them with a prize at the final curtain.

"There is no prize," he said aloud.

On the jukebox, Tom Waits sang about a house on his block with the windows all cracked and no one coming home. "If there's love in a house, it's a palace for sure." Follard wiped his mouth and folded his napkin.

A waitress brought the desserts on a rolling cart. Everything looked old and dry.

"Sad song," he said.

"It's a fucking sad song, if you ask me," said the waitress.

Micah slept, Lyris slept, Charles lay drinking on the davenport. He did not feel like going up. That's how he and Joan used to say it — "Do you feel like going up?" As if they slept in clouds.

16 · Micah

MICAH HAD FALLEN ASLEEP holding a framed picture of Joan. She was waiting for a parade, sunglasses on, fingers tugging thoughtfully on a lock of her silver-blond hair. It was not restful sleep. The air was unbearably dry. He dreamed of lying there awake. And then he was awake, but he could not open his eyes, because their lids had somehow fused. He called for Joan, for Charles, and finally for Lyris.

No one came for the longest time. Dry sand covered his eyes. He wondered what had happened to him, where he had gone, where everyone was. He felt buried alive. He thought of calling out again. If he had landed in some unfamiliar place, maybe it would be better to keep quiet until he knew more. The pillow and blankets were there. Wherever he was, his bed was present.

"What's the matter?" said Lyris.

"I'm blind."

"You're having a dream."

"Look at my eyes."

"Go back to sleep." She switched on the light, turning the darkness pale red. "You do have a problem."

"I think I'm blind, Lyris."

"No, no, no. It's just, you know, what does Joan call it? Stardust."

"It's not stardust," he said. "You don't know what Joan calls anything."

Galvanized by the unfairness of this latest development, he thrashed around the bed. He groaned and growled, dug his heels into the mattress, arched his back like a wild thing.

"Stop it," said Lyris. "That really doesn't help."

She went out, and when she returned, she pressed a hot washcloth over his eyes. It did feel good. His anger melted in the wet heat of the cloth.

"Did this ever happen to you?" asked Micah.

"Yes."

"Where were you then?"

"The orphanage."

"And what did they do?"

"What I'm doing," she said.

Follard assembled the components of a bomb with items found around the house. A stick of incense would be the fuse. He poured some of the kerosene from the blue container into a milk jug. Then he topped off the larger vessel with water, although whom this would fool he did not know.

He parked his car on the WPA road. The jug of kerosene he carried in his right hand. The other devices fit easily into the pockets of his coat. The bomb could be assembled on site in a matter of minutes.

The moon poured light on the ground. He breathed deeply, according to the medical instructions. The sound of his breath filled his ears, as the sound of flames would soon.

Follard moved along through the trees, left leg, right leg, milk jug, over the roots, down the gullies full of wet leaves, toward the Darling place. The barn in which Lyris had been locked would burn to cinders. Someday she would understand.

Follard came down from the trees and into a field of tall brambles. Where was he? The dried burrs waved. He bowed and pushed through the stalks, into a clearing he'd never seen: ruins, moss, and the broad soft leaves of skunk cabbage. The trees began again on the other side of what must once have been a house. He was too far south, that's all he could think. Broken glass glinted on the low walls. A paper target tacked to a dead tree had its heart shot out. He made a note to come back with the metal detector. The coins always fell nearest the house. Follard began to weave, as if he had the metal detector in hand. Then he stopped, hearing a slow creaking sound. The long grass moved unnaturally. Too late, he realized the ground was giving way. Then boards splintered, a wooden platform under the grass, and Follard and his bomb dropped into a hole in the ground.

Micah could see again, but not clearly. He walked to the bathroom and stood at the sink, cupping his hands, filling them, splashing water on his face. When the water got too hot he turned it off and dried his eyes with a towel. Back in his room, Lyris sat in a chair looking at the picture of Joan.

"How's that blindness coming along?" she said.

"It's better than it was."

She handed him his completed homework, an assignment to write questions using words with the *ou* or *ow* sound. "Try reading this."

"What town do you live in, Heathcliff?" he read. "Do you go about bugging people? Why are you so loud, my friend?"

"Now do you believe you can see?"

Micah shut off the light and got into bed. He and Lyris began to talk. They stared at the ceiling, Micah in his bed and

Lyris in the chair, and spoke softly into the darkness. Like siblings who had grown up together, they got down to the true business of parents acting erratically and children responding as best they knew how.

He asked if she would stay now that Joan was gone. She asked where he thought she might go instead. He speculated that since the Home Bringers had brought her to this place because Joan was here, they might now decide to take her to some other place. Lyris said she hoped that would not happen. She said she could not be moving around her whole life. She had moved enough. It occurred to Micah that the Home Bringers might even find Joan and take Lyris to her. Lyris said she could not be forever chasing Joan, and besides, Joan would be coming home in the spring, if what Charles said was true. Micah said Charles could not always be believed and if they were going to keep talking, they should go down and get something to eat. Lyris agreed.

They made a snack tray and went into the living room, where Charles slept on the davenport with a bottle of whiskey and a glass on the floor beside him. Lyris pantomimed waking him, and Micah shook his head. The television was on with no sound. A girl in a black velvet coat was riding a large brown horse over gates and streams. Horse and rider floated at the top of each jump. Once, when the horse veered from a gate, the rider whapped its flank with a stick and circled back for a second try. The horse skidded to a halt, and the rider fell off. Now it was getting interesting. Micah and Lyris sat on a braided rug, eating crackers and watching the rider climb back into the saddle. She had hit her head, but she was no quitter.

Charles mumbled in his sleep, moving his hand slowly beside the davenport. In a dream, he, Micah, and Lyris were at Colette's house, waiting for Joan. She should have been there a long time ago. The kids were watching TV, and Colette was pushing to get supper on. Finally Joan showed up with Jerry. She sat down in a chair in a corner.

"There's your bride," said Jerry. "She's not doing so well."

Charles knelt by her side. Joan smiled, but her face was someone else's, a stranger's face. He asked if she was hungry.

"In a while," she said. "You go on ahead."

Octavia Perry's brother rode with her to the Elephant. He wanted her Grand Am and felt that turning her over to a middle-aged postman in the dead of night was an acceptable price to pay. Jerry had yet to arrive. He and Octavia could not go in her car because of the antitheft tracking device. The grove at the Elephant was desolate against the sky. The brother sensed that his sister was growing up — too fast, maybe, but there you have it. "Just leave the keys in the ignition," he said.

They got out of the car and crossed paths before the hood. Octavia looked at her brother. He was not as handsome as he thought he was. His ears were too small. She hugged him, which felt awkward, since their physical contact had been limited to hitting and pushing for many years. Octavia looked over his shoulder at the valley beyond the Elephant, the separate lights of the farms in the distance.

"Am I making a mistake?" she said.

"I can't answer that, Taff."

She disengaged from the hug, her hands lingering on his forearms. It seemed decent of him not to hustle her off the scene by saying whatever she wanted to hear. In his mind, she knew, he was already behind the wheel.

"Go," she said.

He left. Octavia stood beneath a larch tree, suitcase by her feet. In it she had packed clothes, bracelets, makeup, two sandwiches, and a journal of blank pages. She had never been able to write down her thoughts, which had seemed so run-of-the-mill. Now things would be different.

Her brother stopped a half-mile away. The taillights shone on a hill. Probably he wanted to be sure that her ride would come. He could be very sweet in his way. Her whole family appeared benign, if misguided, in retrospect. Her mother would take it the hardest, would feel so cheated. But November would come, December, snow would fly from the rooftops, and she would know her daughter was gone.

Jerry arrived just when it seemed he would not. He took her hands and held them out and asked her to let him look at her. She wore a CPO coat over a black dress. The wind gusted in the branches.

"Where should we go?" he said.

She pushed strands of hair from her forehead. "Texas?"

"Why there?"

"I heard it was nice," she said softly, the toe of her shoe turning in the grass.

Follard stood in the hole he'd discovered by accident. Anyone without broken ribs could have gotten out. His chin was level with the ground. The hole was lined with corroded metal that had folded down in places to reveal wooden staves behind it. It must have once been a cistern or a dry well. He tried to climb, but the pain made him want to die.

The foxhunters — Vincent, Leo, old Bob, and Kevin — heard his calls while going by the abandoned farm. They followed Kevin's dog to Follard, who could not stop talking. He had given his situation some thought and explained about his ribs and why the obvious solution, pulling him up by the arms, was out of the question. Instead, he said, they should find bricks or rocks to put into the cistern, to serve as steps. He handed up the milk jug to make room.

Leo Miner took the cap off and smelled the kerosene. "What's this for?" He offered the jug around for others to share his discovery.

"I got all the way out here and realized I forgot the fuel for my lantern," said Follard. "I'm camping. So then I had to go back."

"Where's your tent?" said old Bob.

"North of here."

"We just come from north," said Vincent.

"You must have passed it," said Follard.

The foxhunters talked things over. Follard's explanation made some sense, and yet they could not help but suspect that he was up to trouble. He was in no shape, however, to do anything, and they could hardly leave him. They could confiscate the kerosene; they could confiscate Follard himself if they felt like it. Having thus reached a resolution, they began looking around for something for Follard to step up on. The dog ran here and there, not grasping what they were after. No rocks could be pried from the foundation. Those old-time masons knew what they were doing. The hunters gathered again around the cistern, hunkered down. It seemed unbelievable that this man only slightly below them could not be raised to their level. Old Bob offered Follard a drink of schnapps, which he gratefully accepted. Kevin showed him the fox they had killed about an hour ago. It was such a small thing, like a house pet.

"I have an idea," said Leo.

"It'll never work."

"Listen to me, Vincent," said Leo. "What if we take off our coats, tie them together by the sleeves, and form a kind of sling to lift him out?"

"Sure, that will solve it," said Vincent.

"It's worth trying," said Kevin.

"It's cold down here," said Follard.

"You keep out of this."

They tied their coats together. It worked. When Follard was free, everyone stood in silent admiration of Leo's ingenuity. Then Leo picked up the jug of kerosene and carried it out into the clearing. He poured it on the ground at the base of the dead tree with the paper target. Not to be outdone, Vincent tossed a match on the kerosene. The fire seemed to fall from the sky. The tree went up like dry paper.

"That's what I wanted to do," said Follard.

In town, Colette was still awake. She sat in bed, reading a letter she had written to the Bily Clock Museum. She shook her head. All she wanted was to say how much she had enjoyed her visit, but reservations kept creeping in. She tore the letter and tossed the pieces on the floor. There were others down there. Colette put a clean sheet of paper on a breadboard in her lap. *Dear Sir or Madam,* she wrote. *You have a place that is unlike any other. Take care of it. And tell me this: What made those brothers the way they were? Could it ever happen again?*

The riders pinned ribbons to the bridles of their horses. Lyris turned off the television. She stretched, arms lifted and palms up, as if to keep something from falling. A coughing fit seized Micah and he staggered to the boot room, where he would not wake Charles. He rested his arms on the deep freeze and looked out the window. The porch columns, the barn, the tracks, and the trees were all there in the moonlight. How good it felt to not be coughing anymore.

Charles woke anyway and lumbered outside in his stocking feet. He called Micah and Lyris to come see a band of light in the sky. None of them could identify it as the reflection of a burning tree. Through some distortion of the night air, it seemed vast and very far away.

"Must be . . . the aurora borealis," said Charles.

"I don't think so," said Lyris. "It seems to be dying out."

"That is aurora as sure as we're standing here."

"Joan would know," said Micah.

They stayed out a little while longer. The goat lay on the porch, ears back, a placid silver form. Then the moon slipped below the trees and darkness welled over the house, the fields, the woods, and the road. A night bird called, a cat answered, yowling with a hunger that would never go away, and it was quiet.